BORN TO WAR

FUTURE DIVIDE: DAUGHTERS OF WAR

TOMAS BURIAN

PROLOGUE

At the end of the third millennium, two forces are locked in an eternal war in a world full of secrets. What we miss here on Earth exists on the distant world of Sentia in abundance. Magic - the ability to control the forces of nature - exists in every living being. Some have plenty, some have barely worth mentioning. It is an excellent instrument of war, the war dividing the once united people whose home was once Earth.

"We are the People of Edenia, descendants of the Erthe's mages. We carry the nobility of our ancestors in our hearts with pride and dignity. We refuse to bow down to those who proclaimed themselves to be gods and see death before we join their ranks. Freedom is our right and our treasured gift. We will fight to the last to defend it."

- FROM THE INTRODUCTION TO THE KINGDOM OF EDENIA

"We are the children of the one true God who appears to us in two forms. It is our duty to atone for the sins of our forefathers cast out of Erthe. Enlightenment is our gift, salvation is our destiny. Together we must stand and destroy those who want to deny us this honor. With vigilance and courage, we will swipe aside all who stand in our way. Only then will we see Erthe again."

- FROM THE INTRODUCTION TO THE ORDER OF THE NEW GODS

1

CALM BEFORE THE STORM

Streams of white energy flowed around Kordon's head, illuminating him against the gray background. Like a wind of force, they played with his long hair. He felt deaf. No sound existed in the stream world besides that of a spoken word. He looked around, but the only thing he could see was an endless realm of white energy flowing through the darkened space with no beginning or end.

"Samara!" he shouted, his voice echoing across the void. The only answer was silence. "Curious," he thought out loud to himself. He already yelled several times and still there would be no answer.

Kordon and Samara were the Great Sorcerers, humans who had near unlimited magical power and the ability to communicate in the stream world. Although not physically present, their thoughts could be shot from one to another through this immaterial space. It required concentration but allowed them to communicate even when thousand miles apart.

Kordon had hoped Samara would be attuned and able to respond. They could see the stream world inside their minds when they closed their eyes and let themselves loose into it. Whether they would appear visible was entirely up to them and Kordon often chose so. Normally, Samara would respond, but not this time. He looked around, hoping to see her, despite knowing he would always hear her first before she would appear.

He was alone.

"I must not let it bother me now," he thought to himself, teeth clenched in desperation. "My family needs me, my second child is about to be born. And our people need us both, Samara. We must protect them all. So where are you?"

THE LARGE HOTEL BEDROOM WAS PLEASANT, SERENE, AND flooded with the morning sunlight. The sun's warm touch colored the walls of white marble, the purple bedspread and the green leaves of all the plants. Kordon wouldn't let the rising sun wake him up. To him, there was no outside world. He couldn't hear the tweeting of the birds passing by the large windows. During his sleep, he slipped from his dreams into the stream world.

But he wasn't alone in the bed. A gentle push

brought him back to the real world. Kordon woke up as if he was in shock, breathing heavily. Someone's hand startled him by touching his cheek. Looking to his right, he saw Dianne's beautiful face. Despite sleeping on a bed large enough for ten people, his wife was tucked tightly to him. Her shining brown eyes smiled at him, watching him from underneath the blanket they shared.

"Good morning, darling," she whispered to him.

Kordon, with sweat on his forehead, stared at her with confusion.

"I... I shouldn't have woken up." His words felt heavy and troubled. The tone he spoke with was very uncommon of him, something he would only allow in an intimate presence. But Dianne's smile did not waiver.

"Of course you should have. Why not?"

Kordon looked out of the window to greet the sunshine. He hoped to wash away his worries.

"I was waiting for her. She never arrived." He tried to wipe the sweat from his forehead. It was a futile effort.

"Don't let that bother you. It's a beautiful day. Let's get up."

Dianne took the blanket off of them. She got up and undressed her sleeping robe. Kordon watched her. Her blonde hair shone in the sunlight and even with a bloated belly of a pregnant woman, she was still so graceful, so beautiful – maybe more than ever.

He knew it would pass. Her beauty would wither away and disappear forever. He was used to that. After living for so long, it seemed as a fleeting moment to him. Yet this time, her children – their children, will carry a part of her beauty in them. As long as their children live and carry on their legacy, Dianne shall never fade away from his mind - provided he will outlive her. For nearly a thousand years, which were normally called sun cycles, the war kept raging on. And though Kordon never aged, he certainly wasn't immortal. He could be killed and he knew that. So much uncertainty existed in his life, in this world.

Meanwhile, Dianne began putting on her underwear. She noticed how Kordon was watching her. With a smile, she spun around on a heel, displaying her otherwise slender and young body.

Kordon stood up. Wearing only the velvet pants he used for sleeping, he approached Dianne and embraced her from behind. "You're beautiful," he whispered into her ear. "I woke up from a nightmare into a sweet dream." Dianne placed her hand on the back of his head as he kissed her neck. She held him like that for a moment with a smile of pleasure and satisfaction on her lips.

Their stares met inside a nearby mirror.

"Look, a married couple. What a happy family," she said.

"That is what we fight for," admitted Kordon.

"Yes, we fight all our lives. Killing our own people

who just happen to stand on the other side," she said with sorrow in her voice.

"They made their choice to stand with the Gods ever since we discovered them," he stated gently yet with a certain amount of bluntness.

"It doesn't make it any easier for me, Kordon," replied Dianne.

"I'm sorry I made you think of it. I had to watch people die for thousands of sun cycles. It made me see the world differently," said Kordon.

Dianne turned to him and looked him in the eyes.

"You're a man of great burden, my love. As your wife, I share it with you. So, do not be troubled. I will always be by your side and do what I can to support you."

Smile appeared on Kordon's lips.

"I can't be any happier for having you by my side," he said and gently ran his hand across her face. She closed her eyes as she smiled.

"How about we'll get you ready for the day, hmm? We have our kingdom to represent before the local royalty." She put a humorous tone to her last two words, apparently trying to make him both amused and excited.

Kordon smiled and nodded. It was time to get the politics started.

· · ·

Soon after, Kordon and Dianne set out to the castle to meet a special friend. Their chambers were on the opposite side of the city, giving them the opportunity to enjoy the beautiful spring weather.

Kingdom of Hanal belonged to the frontline kingdoms of the Second Continent, always threatened by the attacks of the enemy from the east. Due to this fact, most of the housing in the capital city was situated in its western half. In the eastern half, behind a large fortress wall, stood a massive castle surrounded by storehouses, forges and other military installations. The castle reached for the sky, towering above everything like a protective parent watching over its children.

As Kordon and Dianne advanced through the city, the architecture became different with each block. The streets changed their width one after another to provide bottlenecks for slowing down any invading forces. Everything appeared plainer and sharp-edged, losing its romantic colors to black and grey. Statues of important people and colorful cloths hanging over the streets gave way to orange metal decorations and large blue flags with royal insignia waving in the wind.

"How do you like the city?" asked Kordon, seeing how his wife's eyes shifted and traced every detail around them.

"I have never been here before," admitted Dianne. "But I am imagining things that must have happened here. People here had to endure so much struggle to protect us who live in the west. Life is difficult without our technology that makes life so easy. Even now, when the Gods' curse doesn't disrupt magic, they do not have any of our devices. They just keep to their proven ways."

"It's dangerous to rely on the technology of magic," noted Kordon.

"But I can hardly imagine going back to the life I had growing up. I enjoy the comfort of magic we have back in Edenia," smiled Dianne.

She recalled her current home, Edenia, a large island kingdom, the very first settlement made on this planet. Kordon and Samara founded it after the discovery of the new gods, before the eternal war broke out. It enjoyed plentiness and safety, located many miles off the western coast of the Second Continent where death roamed free and magic had only limited use. While Edenia and the western regions of the Second Continent enjoyed futuristic technology and somewhat comfortable lifestyle, the rest of the known world was submerged in the eternal Middle-Ages.

They held each other's hands as they walked. Surprisingly, they were the only ones in the whole city who did so. Despite that, Kordon still could not put his mind to ease. He would keep walking with his eyes aimed at the ground, silent.

"Why was I chosen to come to Hanal instead of Samara?" wondered Dianne. "If this is a political visit, she is the one of your equal status to represent Edenia."

Kordon nodded in acknowledgement of the idea but shook his head shortly after.

"I don't know. It was clearly stated that you and I are invited. Samara is with her family in New Sevilla, but I don't know why."

"Is that why you were trying to contact her in the stream?"

"That too, but…" Kordon interrupted himself in the middle of a sentence and thought for a moment. "I couldn't get to talk to her for a long time. I'm afraid Danub stepped into the stream again. He might have discouraged her from entering."

Dianne had never met Danub Rey, the man who, just like Kordon, never aged and possessed unlimited magical power. Unlike Kordon, Danub stood on the side of the Gods, being their people's ultimate leader in their name. He believed them and their vision, refusing to ever see a reason in opposing them, a fact that lay heavy on Kordon's heart to this day.

"Your greatest enemy has managed to disconnect you from your greatest ally? Do you think it means he's on the move to recommence the war?"

Kordon closed his eyes in thoughtfulness. "He is not my enemy. Adversary, yes, but we were friends for a long time and he is still one of us, the Great Three. He just chose to stand on the side in which he believes."

"Is he really as vile as it is said?" Dianne's voice carried a hint of fear, rather than curiosity.

"He is a natural born winner and he doesn't take

chances. His devotion to victory is also his weakness. If I happen to win, he breaks down for a long time."

"And you are afraid that such time has passed now?"

Kordon sighed. "I don't want to be in war. I have seen too many people die already."

He felt her grip on his hand tightening, as if she wanted to remind him she's by his side.

"We'll find the way to end this war, together. Good things are coming, I can feel it."

Kordon gratefully smiled at her and then turned his stare forward again.

"It all depends on Samara. She is very crucial to our survival. With our side being outnumbered, she keeps the balance in this war. She must not die."

Dianne stopped and grabbed onto both his hands. "You must not die. What would I do then? What would we all do?"

Kordon smiled. "I have lived long enough."

"Not enough for me," said Dianne with a smile. "And your children will need you," she added as she kissed him on the cheek, summoning a slight smirk on his face.

"Don't worry, I don't plan leaving Naarde any time soon," he said.

"Naarde," repeated Dianne. "No one calls this world that but you."

Kordon smiled. "You are almost correct with the pronunciation. Almost."

"I am trying my best to remember what you have taught me of your language so I can also teach it to our children when they grow up," admitted Dianne.

"And what do you remember so far?" asked Kordon curiously.

Dianne cleared her throat. "Ik woerdar dit maie weere mit minn knapp mann."

Kordon laughed out loud. "Very good! But remember, most of the sound is generated in the throat, not so much on the tongue."

Dianne smirked. "I'm sorry, that's just how my parents taught me to speak so I could speak the language of my ancestors properly."

"And here we are, both speaking Änglish, a language that is not ours!" continued Kordon in laughter.

"I thought Änglish was our language now," wondered Dianne.

"In a way," nodded Kordon. "But we each also have a language not many others understand."

"And since Ifrenchia is now hostile, I don't get to use my mother tongue anymore," added Dianne.

Kordon felt a hint of regret in his wife's voice. He reached out to her and caressed her cheek.

"Don't let the betrayal of your home country discourage you. We didn't bring languages from Erthe to forget them."

Dianne smiled.

"Here you go again, talking about the famed and beautiful Erthe, the jewel of your stories."

"Stories, you say?" laughed Kordon. He remembered well how Dianne could not get enough of his stories about the old world, Erthe, which was no other than planet Earth's name during the time when all mages were exiled from it. Erthe was Kordon's birthplace, as well as Samara's and even though they publicly claimed they had forgotten much of that time, it was far from the truth.

"Well, if that's what you want, then gather around and listen."

Dianne burst into laughter as well.

"No, please. Don't! I won't be able to think of anything else!" she begged him sarcastically, knowing her plea would go unheard. Kordon would keep on walking, fully engaged in his storytelling.

"I come from a small area of Drenthe in Nederland and there we did things differently than here."

Together they would disappear in the crowd.

THEY FINALLY REACHED THE CASTLE. IT SEEMED GIGANTIC from the ground, its effigy-like structure rose to the sky, accompanied by several towers encircling it. Its ivory walls reflected the morning sun, blinding anyone daring to behold its grandeur. Dianne tried to look up to see the top and would have fallen over backwards had Kordon not caught her in time.

"Aren't you also glad it's on our side?" she asked just when she managed to exhale in relief.

"Yes, it would be hard to reclaim it," agreed Kordon.

"Not for you and your power," Dianne said with a smile.

"That's true. But I would be a fool to do it alone," he reminded her.

Soon they strode through the inner hallways. Dianne admired the regal decorations of royal blue curtains and orange gold signatures over the white stone walls. Seeing the clean and well-maintained interior, Kordon smiled slightly with satisfaction. The rigidity of being a frontline kingdom taught the local people to work hard on preserving what they had. It was a great contribution to have Hanal on Edenia's side. They passed along the large windows that let in most of the light coming in from the western side. The eastern side had only very small windows as that was where the attacks always came from. The whole city was built as a defensive structure. Still, the practical architecture did bear many beautiful designs.

Kordon and Dianne were well recognized in the city. Even to people who never met him, his visage declared his status. He wore a white robe with golden plates on his shoulders and a white armored plate on his chest with Edenia's symbol of a stylized letter S decorated his clothes in several places. Dianne too would wear her white robe decorated with embroidery and golden bracers set with jewels glinted on her wrists as she walked through the morning sunlight. Her most recognizable trademark was a beautiful golden circlet with a single spike aiming upwards in the middle of her forehead. As it was a custom, even the decorative clothes were practical and could contain hidden gadgets and tools to help in an eventual combat. Both Kordon's and Dianne's clothes had them, hidden for the right moment to be used for defense. And even though Dianne's boots had high heels, they would not be higher than one inch, allowing for faster movement in case of danger. Such was life in the war-torn world.

Everyone bowed to the great mage and his wife but not as deeply as they had to bow to the king. Kordon didn't mind, though. He was a noble, many times close to the queens and kings, but never a king himself. He knew that a ruler of men had to change so that the next generations would always have space for improvement. It kept the world more in the hands of its people and left Kordon with time to focus on other important things.

* * *

THE GREAT DOORS HAD OPENED AND REVEALED THE observation lounge. This, except for some balconies, was the only room that had a clear view toward the east. The rising sun hung above the mountain range and bathed the valley and the city in its warm light.

Kordon and Dianne entered the room, greeted by the curious and respectful glances of many people. Dianne always felt proud being by her man's side. His very presence demanded respect that only few men in the world could match. He was a Great Sorcerer, which meant that not only he had an unlimited magical power, he also never aged. Everyone in the world would only know him as a man who always looked about forty years old and yet he carried the aura of ageless wisdom and seriousness. Tall, muscular, rugged manly features and his long blonde hair loosely laid on his broad shoulders made him a lion among men she so enjoyed having only for herself. She hoped to never get used to this feeling, wishing for it to ever be so strong as the first time they came to be together.

A woman in light red armor smiled as she approached them. Her long brown hair was tied in the back into two ponytails, running down along her cape as long as her waist. Though she was young and beautiful, she could not quite compare to Dianne, who had just turned thirty sun cycles and would not even look that old.

"Welcome to Hanal, my lord," she said as soon as she was sure Kordon was close enough to hear her over the crowd's chatter. The court's officials quite commonly used the lounge as a place for morning meetings - fairly informal meetings, of course.

Kordon smiled and offered her a hand. The woman bowed down and kissed it. Then her sparkling blue eyes shifted at Dianne. "And your lady," she added and kissed Dianne's hand, too. Dianne smiled a little and bowed her head slightly.

"You enjoy playing courtesies, don't you, Maliana?" asked Kordon, laughing.

"No," answered Maliana, with a devilish smile. "Only enjoy touching people with my mouth."

Dianne looked upon Kordon's face to see how he would react to such a jestful expression, but he remained entertained. Kordon was incredibly old and had heard all that people ever had to say, but it seemed as if he willingly pretended that everything was new to him.

"Oh, I see. Does it work the other way too? The last man that tried to kiss you ended up with his face in the mud."

Maliana gasped in surprise. "Oh, but that was not my fault. He slipped on the very same mud."

Kordon lowered one of his eyebrows. "You kicked him in the shins."

Maliana pressed her lips together and conjured a wide smile. "Well, either way, it's good to see you both."

She turned to Dianne. "It is so long since I have seen you. How is the baby doing?"

"Oh, wonderful. It's moving already. Not as fierce as

the first one, though. I think this one will be more of a tender person," said Dianne.

"Entirely like her mother, huh?" guessed Maliana.

"Maliana, where's Zatrek and Korba? I wish to speak to them as well as the king. Wasn't he to greet us here too?" asked Kordon.

"The king is too busy right now. Perhaps later? As for your friends, I don't know. How can I? I don't track every move of every noble in the kingdom. Recently, I have been busy selecting the new royal guard."

"Ah, you are the one responsible for the soldiers' sortie," realized Dianne.

"Yes, I am actually just a noble officer employed in this kingdom's army. Not a real soldier. But due to our kingdom's position and imminent threat, everyone in the army has to be armored. Oh, and many noble houses will be arriving." She winked at Kordon. "We are having a special surprise there for you, too."

She paused for a moment and bowed. "Now if you will excuse me, I have some errands to run. See you in the evening."

Kordon and Dianne both nodded in agreement as Maliana left the room.

"Something bad is indeed about to happen," pondered Kordon.

"No, it's just that you don't like surprises," said Dianne, entertained.

"They usually turn out unpleasant," replied Kordon folding his hands on his chest. He closed his eyes and wondered what it could be coming his way this evening. Dianne put her hands together as if in a prayer. Then a surprised look appeared on her face.

"Look, it's Ramon Gall. I almost didn't recognize him with the beard," she said, pointing briefly at the other side of the room. A man in a decorated leather armor stood there, golden symbol of Edenian royal guard glinting on the back of his cloak. Although old with gray hair and beard, he was still elegant and handsome, despite the fact that a vicious scar ran across his cheek, which would disfigure any other man, but only added to his battle-weary look.

"How old is he now?" wondered Dianne.

"Nearly sixty sun cycles. Come, let's talk to him," said Kordon.

Ramon noticed them both before they managed to surprise him. He excused his current partner in chat and welcomed the noble pair with a hearty smile.

"My lord, my lady," he said, expressing his welcoming hand gesture. Kordon and Dianne returned the greeting the same way.

"Good to see you here, old friend," said Kordon with a smile.

"Old? Look who's talking. I'm a mere youngster compared to you," said Ramon jokingly.

"Does old time friend sound better to you, sonny boy?" burst Kordon into laughter.

"Fair enough, friend. Fair enough," nodded Ramon, sharing his amusement.

"What brings you here, though? This event seems barely out of ordinary," wondered Kordon.

"I'm the captain of the old queen's royal guard. Although I wasn't invited, I still had to come and check on you."

"Who told you I was here? I do not publish my travels anywhere." Kordon seemed puzzled. He glanced at Dianne, who only shook her head.

"Samara told me," answered Ramon. "I accompanied her to Harij on the old queen's order."

This news disturbed Kordon. He felt Dianne's hand touching his. She could feel his distress. "Samara? What is she up to?" he asked hastily.

Ramon looked at him, a confused look on his face. "She told me you would know."

"And yet I don't," said Kordon, thoughtful. "We will talk about it away from the curious ears. Now, have you spoken to lady Maliana?"

"Yes, I was surprised at how many new guards she had selected. It would do for a whole new squad. We usually don't require that much. Besides, who needs that many guards in the time of peace?" wondered Ramon.

"You need guards to keep the peace. Somebody has to watch over the rogues, greedy nobles, illegal magic research and civil unrest. And do I need to remind you that they help us find the secret forges that provide weapons to anyone willing to spill blood for their own profit?" said Kordon.

"Using the war as an excuse to get rich or get rid of someone. Ah, you're right as usual. As if we haven't hunted enough of those in the past!" agreed Ramon with a tone of disgust.

Kordon quickly glanced around the room. Everyone tended to their own business. Still, he would not take any chances. "Let us take a walk," he suggested.

THEY WALKED IN THE BROADEST STREET LEADING TOWARD THE western exit of the city. Only a few people would be out there at this time. It was easier to make sure that nobody would be able to get close enough to them to eavesdrop.

"So what important business is going on that I don't know of?" asked Kordon.

"The noble house of Moretti has been invited to the same event as you. The same goes for Mondragon and Alves," said Ramon.

"Oh?" That caught Kordon's attention.

"The houses from Harij?" asked Dianne. "That's nice. I wanted to meet them again."

"They weren't supposed to be here," Kordon reminded her. "The local king doesn't get along with them, neighbors or not."

Ramon continued. "Exactly. Samara passed through here on her way to Harij and caught wind of something bad. Now she's there under the pretense of a pleasure visit, you know, to see her husband and friends. In reality, she came there to check on the local noble houses. We are still waiting for any news from her. But I can feel it. Something is about to happen and the noble houses will be involved."

"I have to admit, I was worried before, but this doesn't seem to have any importance to me," proclaimed Kordon. "Noble houses were always unpredictable. If Samara cares about them, it is only her concern."

"Forgive me, friend, but when a web of secrecy looms about you, it never turns out right. You are here alone with your wife and an unborn child. You are too vulnerable."

Kordon shook his head. "I sense no danger here and Samara did not contact me. Maybe she changed her mind. The only thing that concerns me is war. And I'm well confident that with Hanal here and Harij to the south, we have a firm protection. What the nobles do is their problem. You should know by now that I don't get involved in their matters."

Ramon looked at him, rather worried. "Whatever they are up to was enough for one of the Three to look into it personally. I urge you, old friend, do not take this lightly."

Kordon didn't reply. He walked for a moment, thoughts blazing through his mind.

"Very well," he finally spoke. "I'll look into it. Return to the castle and see what you can find."

"What are we going to do?" asked Dianne while watching Ramon disappear among the crowd.

"Samara just made everything more complicated for us," frowned Kordon.

"That is like her, as far as I know," smiled Dianne.

"She's always been like that," agreed Kordon. "Though she can have a bright moment, once in a century."

Dianne giggled.

"I will never get tired of when the immortals make fun of each other."

"She might surprise us yet. Although her absence in the stream worries me. I need to know what she's up to."

"Well, if you can't reach her, then we have to follow her footsteps and maybe we'll find out," said Dianne.

Kordon nodded.

"Let's go visit some old friends."

House Edon's manor sat by the edge of the city, surrounded by a tall wall. The large wooden gate was shut. Nothing indicated life of any kind around or inside the premises, save for two guards standing in front of it, watching everyone who would pass by with suspicious eyes.

"These are not their guards," noted Kordon as they both watched the gate from a safe distance. He stood there, squinting, his arms folded over his chest, letting the wind blow his hair into his face.

"What does that mean?" Dianne asked.

"Let's find out."

The guards watched them approach before they were even within hearing distance.

"Greetings," said Kordon before they even stopped.

"Lord Elenius," one of the guards replied, his look just as stern as Kordon's.

"Lord Edon has his own guard. Why is the city guard stationed here?" inquired Kordon.

"The noble house fell from the king's grace and the property was confiscated."

"Are they kept inside? What have they done?" asked Dianne.

"That is all I can tell you," the guard answered to her.

Kordon and Dianne looked at each other. Neither of them could come to any conclusion yet.

"I wish to go in, step aside."

The guard remained unmoved.

"Nobody enters, no exceptions," was the firm answer.

"You would deny a Great Mage, the leader of all our people, to visit his fellow lord?" asked Dianne, both surprised and upset.

"King's orders, we are honor-bound to obey unless given a direct order from him," explained the other guard.

Kordon frowned and crossed his hands on his chest.

"You do well to abide by the law, but did you know my word supersedes that of all kings?"

"I only answer to the king. I do not make up the rules," answered the guard, rather annoyed.

"Then you won't mind if we break them," said Dianne with a smile and before they could say another word, she pulled something from her bracer and hit the guard closest to her in his temple. He immediately fell unconscious.

Kordon reacted by grabbing the other man's arm. As soon as he had done that, the guard collapsed to the ground as well.

"Go to sleep, my friend," he said and looked at Dianne who gave him an apologetic look.

"Sorry, you know I can be a bit... impulsive sometimes."

"You are my wife, I would be a fool if I didn't see this coming," said Kordon with a smile. Indeed, Dianne was not just a wife to show around. She went through poverty and the death of her family, witnessed the horrors of war and yet she kept a positive approach, playful attitude and honestly loved her husband. Most importantly, however, she had a mind of her own about many things and never feared to break rules for Kordon and his well-being.

Kordon looked at the unconscious men. "Come, we better drag them inside. Even then, we won't have much time before someone realizes they are missing."

They opened the gate with a key found on one of the guards and dragged the bodies inside. The house seemed serene, not a trace of anyone alive in the garden and all the windows were closed.

Kordon knocked on the main door. There was no response.

"Something is wrong," he told Dianne. She could feel his unease. Kordon was a man with a firm sense of order and if something indeed was wrong, proof would never elude him.

"Let us take a look," she replied and was about to approach the door when Kordon halted her with his hand, stopping her from taking another step.

"We don't know who or what we find in there."

Dianne put her hand on his.

"You forget who stood by you in the worst blood-bath you have experienced in my life."

His cold blue eyes met her mellow brown. The way she looked at him, it always felt like it was the first time. She had something in that look that calmed him down.

"You didn't carry a child then," he reminded her, trying to resist her charm for this rare moment.

Dianne knew he was right. It was like that most of the time. His truth could sometimes hurt people and even the untold millennia of his life couldn't completely make him adjust to other people's personalities. To ever convince him otherwise always required proof and logic. However, as his wife, she was a bit more "under his skin", so to speak. She gently took his hand.

"They were guarding a confiscated house. I doubt they would let anything dangerous stay in there. Besides, where else am I safer than by your side?"

Kordon paused for a moment to give it a thought.

"Stay close to me," he said and opened the front door.

"Always," Dianne smiled.

Only when they entered the actual manor they bore witness to the truth behind the serenity. The main hall and all the hallways hosted a rubble of broken furniture and appliances. The curtains and paintings were torn and shards of glass and porcelain littered everywhere among them. The entire house was colored with an eerie light green tint.

Dianne took a closer look at the rubble.

"Is that...?" she asked, surprise and horror in her voice.

"Yes," nodded Kordon. He ran his hand across the surface of a broken table, then lifted it, stained with drying blood. It was splattered everywhere across all the rooms and the bloody smears dragged across floors in all directions.

"Must have been recent," noted Kordon.

Dianne carefully looked at the rubble. Bothered, she turned to Kordon.

"How come there are no bodies?"

Kordon took a deep breath. He squinted as he felt

something itching in his throat. It gave ache to his lungs that desperately struggled to find any oxygen in the inhaled air.

"There is something in the air," he noted sharply.

Diane nodded, wiping sweat from her forehead.

"Do you feel it, too? I thought it could be the bacteria from the blood but it could not have spread so quickly."

Kordon snapped his fingers, a spark that he created ignited the air around it, coloring the air around it yellow.

"Poison," said Dianne, letting out a pronounced cough.

"We should leave, now," Kordon decided.

"If we do, we will never know what happened here," Dianne objected.

"I will not have you risk your lives right now," he insisted.

She looked around, nodding towards the windows.

"We can let it out, think of something."

She quickly approached the closest window and managed to partially open it when Kordon took her hand to stop her.

"No, we are leaving now. There is no life here and if there is anything bound to happen, this place won't tell us."

Dianne stared into his eyes, he returned the stare, adamant and unwavering.

Before Kordon managed to pull his thoughts

together, a sound of irregular footsteps sounded from behind the door to their left. Then it suddenly stopped, followed by a slam, as if something hit the wooden floor.

"We shall make this quick," he said to Dianne, who nodded back at him.

They made for the door, Kordon slam-opened it in a hurry. Before them, just a few yards from the door, lay a girl in a blood red dress, her long black hair covering her head. She lay face down, as if she had fallen while walking toward the door.

Dianne hurried to her, immediately turning her over to check for life signs.

"She's still alive," she looked up at Kordon. "Barely."

They stormed out of the manor's main door, Kordon bearing the girl in his arms. He laid her down in the grass, supporting her head with a flat rock.

"Let's see how bad it is, she might still clear out," said Dianne and knelt next to her.

"Her name is Korin, she is Zatrek Edon's daughter," said Kordon.

Dianne compassionately put her palm on the girl's cheek.

"She must have breathed much more of the gas than us."

"Can we save her?" asked Kordon.

Dianne checked the girl's pulse, then opened her mouth and eyes.

"The infection doesn't seem so severe, but she is

unconscious. It's impossible at this moment to tell what the poison was designed to do. If she was still alive and moving when we entered the manor, there might still be time to bring her back."

"At this moment she might be too important to let her die," Kordon reminded her.

"Oh, you would ask too much from this field medica. I'm used to stab wounds, fractures, bruises... I have very little poison experience," said Dianne quickly in panic.

Suddenly, she stopped.

"She's not breathing."

She pressed her ear to the girl's chest.

"Her heart is still beating. Something must be blocking the air from inhaling."

"Maybe it's designed to make people choke to death," noted Kordon.

"Maybe, her body wants to breathe but can't. Something is blocking the tracheatic passage. Most likely her trachea is swollen," said Dianne and pulled a needle-shaped object from her bracer.

"First I will puncture the trachea as close to her lungs as possible, then we see if there is something to be done about the blockage."

She removed the largest round gem from her bracer and unscrewed a golden tip attached to it. A clear liquid poured out as she put it over the girl's chest, right over where a gap would be between her ribs.

Then she lifted the needle-like object towards Kordon.

"Would you, please?"

Without saying a word, Kordon reached for it with his fingers but stayed his hand just an inch away from it. Dianne felt the intense heat on her fingers as the object became covered by fire for a brief moment.

"Wish me luck. If I do this wrong, I will stab her in the heart instead," said Dianne with a slight worry.

"You are her best hope," said Kordon.

Her eyes focused, she ran the needle across the skin until she was sure it was the right spot.

"Inserting now," she said and punctured the girl's skin with the sterilized tip. The needle's hollow tip buried itself deeper and deeper as Dianne drove it towards the trachea.

"There, we are in," she said, feeling the heartbeat with her other hand. She detached a large gem from her other bracer. After opening its tip, she attached it to the needle.

"You believe that mydion will help to clear her inside?" asked Kordon.

"I have seen it do some amazing things, Kordon. It is the best chance to go on now. Let's wait and see if we learn something new," answered Dianne while attaching the gems back to her bracers.

She smiled lightly as she watched the girl's chest slowly rise and sink, taking in the air through the hollow needle.

Kordon put his hand on her shoulder as they both patiently watched the girl for any change. She put her hand over his.

The girl gasped, almost as if by a reflex. She coughed out a small cloud of blue gas, the remains of mydion, Dianne's universal healing liquid. Her breathing became much fuller and regular although there were no signs she had come to yet.

With great relief, Dianne pulled the needle out of the girl's chest. She lifted her smiling face up to Kordon.

"Making wonders without magic."

Kordon returned the satisfied smile. He felt proud of his caring and intelligent wife. In the time nobody could see past her beauty, he recognized her amazing character and gave her the opportunity to realize her potential. Now she was a living embodiment of the faith he had in her.

"Please, tell me you are there," said Dianne and with the movement of her fingers she slapped the girl's cheek a couple of times.

They remained motionless for the next few seconds. Dianne anxiously waited for any signs of improvement.

The girl's head moved, tilted to the side slightly, her mouth opened a little more, letting out a faint growl.

"Korin, wake up," Kordon said slowly, with a calm but commanding tone in his voice.

As if by some spell, the girl opened her eyes, her pupils constricted as she stared into the bright sky.

She immediately looked at Kordon, meeting his

calm look with a piercing gaze. Slowly, her eyes moved towards Dianne and the happy expression on her face.

"My lord, my lady," she said slowly with a tone of a newly awoken person.

"Can you move?" asked Dianne, concerned.

The girl answered by moving her fingers at first, clutching them into a fist, then relaxing them again. She tried to sit up, but her muscles gave up and she laid back down, having her head supported by Dianne's hand.

"Easy, you were poisoned, we had to bring fresh air back into your lungs. It will hurt to breathe for some time but you will live," explained Dianne.

"Thank you. But..." She coughed a couple of times before managing to continue. Her eyes suddenly widened and Dianne felt the grip on her hand tighten.

"You have to leave. You might be in danger!"

"Tell us what happened," said Kordon.

"Please, listen to me! We are not safe here! Did you see what happened inside? What if someone finds us here?"

She looked to the gate while shaking Dianne's hand even stronger.

"I will deal with it," Kordon reassured her. "Now speak. What did you see?"

"Only violence. These men broke through the door and started killing everyone. I managed to hide, only heard the screams, the noise. Everybody was home then, we even had guests. They didn't spare anyone," she said with tears in her eyes.

"What do you remember of the men who came? Was there anything special about them?" inquired Kordon.

"They were the king's men, the royal guard," answered the girl, overcome with anxiety.

Kordon and Dianne looked at each other.

"I stayed hidden while they murdered my family, hoping they won't find me. But they stayed for too long and I fell asleep," recalled the girl with tears in her eyes.

"The guards outside said that your family was condemned as traitors," said Kordon.

"That can't be true!" the girl cried.

"Maybe there was something we don't know about," guessed Dianne.

"No, you don't understand. I am absolutely sure my family didn't betray anyone."

"What makes you say that?" asked Kordon, rather intrigued.

"Samara Galaxia."

That name brought Kordon some relief.

"So she was here," he said while nodding his head.

"Yes," said Korin. "I was not present most of the time but I remember her saying this: 'I must go to Harij before it's too late. Elenius is coming, he will help you stop the traitors here. He will know everything I know before he arrives.' Those were her final words before she left yesterday morning."

"She trusted them," Kordon thought out loud. "And the king trusted Samara's judgement. It does not make sense he would send his guard to kill them."

"Don't forget that poison gas," said Dianne. "They wanted to be sure that nobody would leave the house."

"Yes, that terrible smell," recalled Korin. "I heard you coming in, wanted to see who it was, but I could not concentrate. My head..."

"What else did Samara say?" asked Kordon.

"I... I remember only a little. I heard her talk about some big change coming, because you two as leaders had failed us and that you and her found the way out of..."

She paused, her eyes racing, as if she tried to comprehend something that made no sense to her.

"Out of what?" asked Dianne, who leaned closer to her.

"The way out of this world," finished Korin.

"What?!" uttered Kordon through clenched teeth.

Dianne looked at him and witnessed his angered face.

"Was she talking about... going back to Erthe?" guessed Dianne.

"Speak of it no more," commanded Kordon in all seriousness.

Dianne turned to Kordon and stood up to face him.

"Kordon, what is this about? Is there something you are not telling us?"

"No," he answered with a stern face. "Samara is crazy."

Dianne was taken aback with it.

"So you say she made it all up? She is your equal. And as far as I know her, she does not go around making people believe in nonsense."

"I'm afraid you'll have to ask her," Kordon simply stated, evading the question altogether. "We will see the king in the evening. At the very least, there will be some explaining for him to do."

"And you," he turned to Korin. "Leave the city, travel west as far as you can. Recover wherever you can, the noble houses will not refuse you."

* * *

LATER THAT EVENING, THE CELEBRATION HAD BEGUN IN THE castle. It took place in the high chamber overlooking the whole city. Many people were already present when Kordon and Dianne arrived. It felt like a display of art, the walls were covered with paintings of important people and tapestries and among the columns stood statues and tall flower pots with plants. Even the people covered themselves in decorated robes and dresses interlaced with precious metals and gems.

The guests enjoyed plenty of food being served and the musicians played slow formal melodies that suited the purpose of a background for chatter.

"I'm still worried about Korin. I wish we could do

something more for her," said Dianne as they walked through the crowd.

"Me too, but I trust your judgement that she will be able to survive the trip long enough to be treated," said Kordon.

"I wonder what it could be that Samara thought you knew," continued Dianne.

"Since she didn't appear in the stream world I suppose we will never know," said Kordon and looked around.

In between the crowd, he spotted Maliana. Even then, she wore the same red robe and cape with light armor over it.

Kordon went ahead and engaged many of the guests in pleasant conversation. Perhaps things weren't so bad after all. Still, he couldn't get to spot some of his missing friends in the crowd. He couldn't let go of his intuition telling him the same fate might have befallen them like Zatrek's family.

Even though he wasn't on the guest list, Kordon insisted that Ramon would be let in as an important figure in the Edenian military. He remained close to the door and observed the gathering.

"So many people. Yet quite short on some familiar faces, don't you think?" asked Dianne when she finally managed to catch up with her husband. But he seemed calm.

"Perhaps they are still going to arrive. I would hate to think something had happened to them as well. But

I would have expected the king to be here. Excuse me for a moment." Kordon set out to get a hold of Maliana.

"Pleasant times, my lord!" toasted Maliana with a smile.

"When will the king appear? It seems that everything is in order now," asked Kordon.

"Maybe you should ask him," said Maliana, nodding toward the other end of the room, where the king's only son, Prince Roland, stood.

The young upstart monarch was hard to overlook. Even now, Kordon could hear his loud laughter quite easily. Even without his status, he would have attracted quite a crowd with his good looks and flamboyancy. Although not quite that muscular, he was tall and his slightly gaunt face sidelined by long dark hair always displayed a wide smile and shining green eyes. The time had come to test his manners.

"I shall," agreed Kordon, and without a word, he turned around and headed toward the prince.

"Kordon." Someone grabbed his hand. He turned around to see Dianne. Her face was twisted in pain.

"What is it, my dear?" he asked in a hurry, concerned about his wife's problem.

"The pain. I think it's something about the baby. It hurts. I need to get to the infirmary." Kordon nodded. He was about to lead Dianne to the infirmary himself, but it wouldn't be quite proper to leave now. Still, he couldn't ignore his beloved's pain.

He looked around. There was only one man he would trust with her.

"Ramon, please take Dianne to infirmary."

"At once, my lord," agreed Ramon as he carefully took Dianne's hand to lead her away. They both left for the exit, but the guard stood in the way and wouldn't let them through.

"I'm sorry, milord, but no one is allowed to leave the room."

Ramon didn't seem to be surprised, yet.

"Out of my way, this woman needs medical assistance."

"Again, I'm sorry but these are my orders. The prince didn't want anyone to leave the room at this time, regardless of circumstances," answered the guard urgently, as he held up his halberd to bar the entire space around him.

"Listen to me, she is a very important noble. You don't want to know what happens if she becomes hurt," tried to explain Ramon, slightly irritated now.

"Everyone in here is somewhat important, milord, but the orders of the prince can't be overridden by anyone other than himself."

Ramon, instead of answering, had to hold Dianne and prevent her from falling to the floor in pain. He gave the guard a strict look.

"Do I have to kill you to get through?"

The guard knew that the captain wasn't joking. It was a tough decision. Ramon didn't give him any more time to think, though. With a swift and precise punch in the face the captain of the Edenian royal guard took the guard out and immediately began to proceed, leaving curious looks behind them.

"Prince Roland, you have some explaining to do. What will you tell me?" said Kordon, rather to himself, while watching the young prince from afar.

He decided to step in. Roland was now standing by the window, looking at his city. He turned around as he noticed Kordon's reflection in the glass.

"Lord Elenius!" he exclaimed as if he was greeting his best friend in the world. Apparently, he meant to avoid any formalities men in such positions had to carry out.

"You look well for being... how old exactly?"

"I don't age," Kordon reminded him.

The prince's eyebrows sank down and his grin disappeared as he pressed his lips together.

"Of course. You're living a dream of staying forever young. I hope you're enjoying the ceremony."

Kordon slightly nodded, studying the real face behind the prince's friendly grin that reappeared before his last sentence. "Yes, I do. But to be honest, I have expected the presence of his majesty, the king."

"Ah yes, I know you two are good friends. Actually, my father doesn't feel very well. He may not appear," explained the prince.

"Hmm, unfortunate," said Kordon with a troubled

frown. He was about to speak again, but the prince was faster.

"And how is your lady doing, if I may ask? I can't seem to spot her anywhere in the crowd," asked Roland, while taking glimpses around the room.

"She had some medical trouble and had to be escorted to the infirmary. It is quite common in such a late stage of pregnancy," said Kordon.

"I see. I hope it is nothing serious. Let me tell you, it is an honor to have her here along with you. She is the last of the great house of Macorsair, isn't that true? Your new offspring will make a great contribution toward the extension of the noble lineage."

"Along with the one we already have, yes. But little Wealla was sick so she had to stay home in Edenia," explained Kordon. He started to feel quite comfortable in this conversation, which alarmed him even more. "I just didn't have a clue that Dianne would get into trouble at the time the ceremony was about to start."

"Most unfortunate. She will miss the surprise we have prepared for you, but I'm sure she will get to know about it, as well."

"Let's skip to the matter, then. Shall we?" suggested Kordon.

The prince reacted with yet another wide smile.

He signaled a servant to bring over a plate of two drinks. He took one and offered the other to Kordon who accepted without hesitation.

"Start the ceremony!" he commanded the adminis-trators.

A rather corpulent old man with a bald head and long gray goatee stepped up on the podium before the windows. He lifted his golden staff and hit the ground with it three times. The music stopped playing and everyone turned their attention to him.

"Honored guests, as a part of this ceremony, we introduce the new members of the royal guard for Edenia, as is a longstanding tradition in our kingdom. Picked as the best of the best, these elite warriors each stand for hundred ordinary men. I am proud to present them to you now."

With a jovial gesture, he waved his hand toward the main entrance, which had then opened. A group of six warriors in shiny metal armor entered, walking in a row, two at a time. They already wore the helmets with a tiger mask but not the royal blue cape. That was only to be given by the queen. All of them lined up before the podium.

The crowd became silent in anticipation. Even the announcer remained silent and only watched quietly.

"And now," he finally spoke, "our lordship prince Roland will have a few words for the introduction of a special surprise."

* * *

RAMON AND DIANNE RUSHED THROUGH THE CASTLE'S corridors as fast they could. Dianne, twisting in pain, relied on Ramon's support. He helped her to descend the massive stairway to the military infirmary in the southern wing of the castle. Just before they could walk through the entrance, Dianne stumbled and fell to the ground. "The pain," she said, holding onto her stomach.

"Almost there, my lady," said Ramon, as he helped her stand. A series of footsteps sounded from behind them.

"You there, stop!"

Ramon turned around. The king's guards stood there. Three of them, approaching slowly, now that they had their attention.

"What's the matter? The lady needs medical attention now!" explained Ramon, holding Dianne so she wouldn't fall again.

"You weren't supposed to leave the ceremony, sir," said one of the guards.

"What are you talking about? We don't have time for this!" Ramon's voice already carried an angry tone. He was not used to anyone consistently trying to stop him from his duties.

"You have to die, sir. Both of you. The prince's order," answered the guard, as all of them drew their swords.

* * *

With a loud applause, the prince stepped onto the podium.

"For a long time, our kingdom has been a solid rock which always stood in the way of its enemies." He paused for a moment to have this fact sink in. "We provided protection to the land and the ruler of Edenia. And we paid the high cost. So many of our people have died. The cities have been demolished, many cultural monuments have been lost. But we have survived! We have rebuilt."

Many heads in the crowd nodded to his words.

The prince's eyes fell upon Kordon. "Lord Kordon Elenius of Edenia, would you step up, please."

Kordon, who so far took a careful note of the new guards, looked at him in surprise. There was no telling what the prince meant, so he obliged. He stepped into the clearing before the podium. Everyone's look rested upon him now.

"My lord, long time ago, before all of us saw the light of day, you defied the new gods and started a rebellion against them. You wanted to free us from their grasp. You started the war, united the kingdoms and led us all ever since. For that, I, on behalf of everyone in my kingdom, thank you."

He lifted his goblet and toasted towards Kordon who briefly smiled and did the same in return. They both took a sip, although Kordon didn't let his eyes away from the prince.

"However," continued Roland, "our kingdom has

endured the merciless barrage of the Gods and their army. We have sacrificed so much and what did we get? So many of our people perished, our cities in ruins."

"You had the privilege of living as free people," answered Kordon, firmly. There was no doubt or hesitation in his voice. Nobody could doubt he was sure of it.

"No! All we gained was death and destruction. Too long have we suffered, but I say, no more."

He gestured to the new guard who took up their weapons and formed a circle around Kordon.

"We are finished with Edenia. We are joining the Gods' holy war. To protect ourselves from your foolish plans that cost us lives. We must do this."

Kordon would not believe that. He did not give anyone satisfaction to see him surprised.

"Is that the king's decision as well?" he asked calmly.

The prince offered him a brief self-satisfied smile. "We removed him, first from his status, then for good from this world. He always talked about how he supported you. Oh, the pride he took in it! So I got rid of him. In fact, we got rid of everyone who opposed my decision. But I'm sure you already know that."

Kordon frowned. "You think you can just take the kingdom? You can't be serious."

"I'm deadly serious, Kordon. Now die!"

Silence befell the room, Kordon defiantly crossed his hands on his chest.

"Why is he still alive? He should've been on his

knees by now!" the prince asked his servants, both surprised and infuriated.

"Do you think I would live this long if it was so easy to poison me with a drink?" asked Kordon with a hint of annoyance.

The prince pointed at him.

"I saw you drink it! How can it be? You are mortal just like us!"

Kordon raised his goblet, then turned it upside down, instead of the regular red, the drink spilled on the floor was now blue.

"I recognized the smell of the poison you used in Zatrek Edon's house and neutralized it with a healing liquid when you weren't looking. Courtesy of my wife."

"No matter! You have walked into our trap!" seeped the prince through the clenched teeth. "Neither you, nor your wife are walking out of here alive. We will end your lineage here and now."

"You wouldn't dare," said Kordon, his eyes flashing with magic. He looked around.

"Yes, we would, Kordon," said Maliana. "We have already sent the guards to dispose of Dianne. She's dead by now."

The magic glow vanished from Kordon's eyes. "Why, Maliana? Why join them? Dianne was your friend, too," he asked with a genuine concern.

Maliana just smirked.

"We never realized that all the Gods wanted to do was to unify our people into one solid nation. They eventually will. We can't hold them off forever. I'm sorry that you and Dianne have to die, Kordon, but you have brought that upon yourself. You can't oppose the Gods who rule over an army bigger than all of us."

"Yes we can, the Gods can be destroyed. If we are united then we can win this war," insisted Kordon but Maliana interrupted him.

"This war? What do you even know about the war? You're just hiding behind our lines while our people, real men and women stand and die, over and over. Two thousand cycles and nothing has changed for better. It's just our people who stand up and have a sword run through them. For you, coward!"

There was a moment of silence to let the truth sink in.

"You said there is no one here who would support Edenia," said Kordon, as if he was trying to remind himself.

"Indeed," agreed Roland.

"Then I don't need to have any regrets about killing you all," Kordon said as he lifted his hand to release his magic upon everyone.

But the prince spoke before he could manage to do so. "Don't jest yourself, Kordon. You may overpower us here, but you are not invincible. One strike is all it takes. You will not escape."

Kordon smiled slightly. "I can try."

Roland sighed. "Why don't you look out the

window," he said and pointed toward the large windows on the eastern side of the room.

Kordon approached them slowly, still watchful of the people surrounding him. They seemed strongly confident, though. Even Maliana stepped aside, letting him pass through. Looking outside, he could see the eastern great gate wide open and through it, an army marching right into the city streets. The enemy had arrived and nobody was there to fight him. Maliana carefully approached Kordon.

"We let them in, Kordon. You are completely surrounded. Nobody is going to help you." Kordon didn't ask anything anymore. He already knew. He wondered, should he stay and try to take down as many of them as he could, or just flee and warn the Edenian forces?

Suddenly his body froze with one thought; Dianne, he had to get to Dianne.

"If the war should return," he said, without taking his look away from the outside, "you shall be the first to fall."

With lightning speed, Kordon reached for Maliana, and before she could react, he slammed her into the window. The glass broke, and as Kordon released her, Maliana flew out. Kordon didn't even bother watching her disappear in the depths of the cityscape. Her scream faded away just as fast as any good memories he had of her.

"Kill him! Don't give him a chance to attack!" he heard the prince shout, as he turned around.

The next thing he saw was a shot from a crossbow, aimed at his heart.

While still in motion, Kordon managed to dodge it partially, and the bolt pierced his shoulder protector, its point emerging on the other side.

He groaned in pain as the pressure of the impact made his shoulder snap back. The knights were already upon him. They didn't leave any space for him to pass through.

There was only one way out, through the hole in the window. But the room was on the twelfth floor and the castle's wall was completely flat on the outside. He would have nothing to grab on to.

Two seconds left. Time to decide.

* * *

"What is this? What are you talking about?" asked Ramon, consistent in his anger.

His surprise couldn't compare to Dianne's, however. Even through her pain she understood what was happening but she didn't understand why.

"Put your weapon aside and get down on your knees, both of you," the guardist demanded. Ramon knew that the man wasn't joking.

"My lady, get into the infirmary and lock yourself

in. I will hold them back," he said to Dianne, as he drew his own sword.

Dianne could barely recover from the shock. What was this about? A friendly invitation to the ceremony. Was it a ruse? And what of Kordon? He was in peril.

Ramon turned back to the guards. "You want me? Try to take me!" he shouted.

The swordplay had begun. Ramon blocked the attack of the first guard and then tackled another who was trying to catch Dianne. He managed to run his sword right through the opening in the man's armor, instantly killing him.

Dianne put all her effort into moving as fast as possible. The nearest door was nearly twenty feet away. Clenching her teeth, she ignored the pain and pushed her body to the limit. She heard Ramon dealing with the other two guards, but didn't want to look behind. Her heart beat like crazy, her breath was heavy. Her head felt as if it were under a huge pressure, and her forehead started to sweat. She focused on a single thing, getting into the infirmary room as quickly as possible.

A sound of another guard dying reached her ears as she neared the door. A few more steps got her inside the room. She immediately tried to push the wooden door shut. Struggling to breathe, she clung onto her fading strength, and attempted to lock herself in the room. She succeeded. Only then, she could turn around and collapse to the floor. It was quiet. No more sounds came from the outside.

"My baby," she whispered, keeping her hand on top of her stomach. Her respite, however, lasted only a moment. A mighty blow struck the door. It held. Another one. Dianne watched in fear as an iron gauntlet struck through the wood, splintering it. Then a blade came through, shattering more of the door. Dianne looked around. A nearby shelf had a guard's gear on it, including a sword. She crawled toward the shelf and reached for the sword.

"I do this for you," she said, unsheathing it. Then she stood up and approached the door, which was about to be broken from the outside. She lifted the weapon above her head and drove it through the door with the remainder of her strength. A deadly scream came from the other side. Dianne left the sword where it pierced the door and collapsed to the floor again. She sat up against the wall while breathing heavily, occasionally gasping for air.

"There will be more, certainly," she told herself. A feeling of despair took over her mind. They would find her soon and kill her and the baby. She can't let that happen. But what could she do? Only death awaited her behind the door. Perhaps she could crawl out through the window. But not in this condition.

* * *

SOUNDS OF FIGHTING CAME FROM THE OUTSIDE, FOLLOWED BY deadly screams of men.

Dianne looked up. Through the open window she heard someone running, the sound of footsteps kept closing in. Were they after her? She hid behind the table and peeked out. For a second she saw someone running past the window, someone dressed in a white and gray robe with long blonde hair.

Could it be?

Dianne couldn't believe her eyes but she knew it was true. She immediately leaped from behind the table using all the strength she could muster.

"Kordon! Kordon!" she shouted as much as her lungs allowed her. She held onto the tables, chairs and everything to get to the window. Her legs shook and barely supported her. The pain still didn't let her go but that was all irrelevant now.

There was no more sound coming from the outside. The street reeked of emptiness by now. Dianne couldn't hear or see anyone. Her only hope was to get to her husband.

She was almost at the window when someone appeared in it. Dianne was taken aback until she realized it was Kordon. The dark world became a little brighter and hope started to grow again.

"Dianne!" he said. "You're alive. I can't believe it." He reached out for her and helped her climb through the window. His hands were covered in blood but he seemed unharmed.

"Kordon, my love!" she cried and held tightly onto him.

"We have to get out of here. It's an insurrection. Where is Ramon?" asked Kordon and looked around.

"They killed... they killed him," was the answer.

"They will soon know we are here. We have to leave this place and return to Edenia," said Kordon and led Dianne away while supporting her. They took the next turn right around the corner and entered a door leading to an underground corridor.

"How do we hide from them?" asked Dianne but Kordon led her deeper into the underground without a word.

Finally they stopped in the middle of a lightless corridor illuminated only by Kordon's magic light. "I helped to build this city. There are many secret tunnels."

He carefully laid Dianne on the floor and turned around. Then he picked up a pair of steel hooks from the wall and wiped the dust where the wall touched the ground. There were two small holes there. Kordon inserted the hooks and pulled upwards. The whole wall rose up revealing another corridor leading somewhere far into the darkness.

"Kordon..." Dianne's voice came from behind him but faded away quickly. Kordon turned around to see her faint. He immediately knelt next to her and carefully lifted her up. After he walked through the opening the wall slid back down.

They were in a complete dark now. Kordon put Dianne over his left shoulder and lifted his right hand up to make it shine with a magical light. The corridor was completely empty and straight. Its ending disappeared somewhere in the darkness.

"Stay with me, my dear. I will get you to safety," he said and set out on a long walk.

2

DESPERATE ESCAPE

It was a good half an hour trip in the empty, narrow corridor and Kordon couldn't tell how much longer it would be. The air felt quite putrid and damp. Even he had trouble breathing properly in there.

In a way, he was glad that Dianne was unconscious. She needed rest and being in this state made it easier for her to deal with this horrible air.

It seemed to him that the way had been turning to the north slightly, as it led him behind the mountain range. Nothing could be found there besides miles and miles of a dense forest. It wasn't very populated, except for some farmers, wild animals and perhaps some groups of rogues. It made sense, actually. If the city was invaded, nobody would be able to easily cross the mountains to look for the escapees.

The walk seemed endless, but all that time Kordon couldn't let his mind off of what had happened. The betrayal touched him on a personal level. He was the first one to see through the ruse of the so-called Gods. As the prince stated, Kordon had instigated the uprising against them and united the kingdoms for his cause. For centuries, men and women fought and died for freedom, but still more and more left to join his enemies.

Kordon knew that life in the universe had a creator. It was a part of his history he never spoke of. And he was absolutely sure that these beings weren't like him.

Nearly two millennia ago, the newly arrived mages expanded to the Second Continent, where they discovered the Black Pyramid. There they met the two beings who claimed to be two aspects of God; the Destroyer and the Creator. Those who tried to deny them were slain by them personally, the beings shrouded in light, indestructible. Those who followed were promised deliverance from this world, the return to Earth, eternal life and the magic powers just like Kordon and the other Three. But in order to achieve deliverance, all resistance had to be eliminated.

He couldn't stop thinking of what he should do. He needed to warn the other kingdoms, he was their leader. Even though he left them autonomy, they chose to follow him. With Hanal taken over and Harij under siege, it left the front open. If the enemy took advantage of it, he would be to blame.

And yet he couldn't stop thinking about Dianne. He needed to protect her. He was her husband, her safety came first. It tore him apart on the inside ever since he married her. Being a father and a husband while also leading entire nations split his focus. He was never afraid of responsibility. He wanted it, he wanted to lead and in marriage his own mentality failed him. Although nobody could say he hadn't tried, he knew others in the similar position and hoped to avoid doing the same mistakes they had done. But no one was precisely like him, stress upon him was thousandfold compared to anyone save for Samara who only managed to escape accountability by putting it on Kordon.

It was his responsibility that the baby would be born without difficulty. Should Dianne miscarry due to this stressful situation, it would be a tragedy for both of them. He always wanted to have two children. If he and Dianne died, there would be someone else to replace them. It intrigued him, what if their children also would not age? What could they achieve? And would they survive the war? He couldn't wait to find out.

Then he reminded himself to stick to the present. He was in danger, Dianne was in danger. The whole world he struggled to preserve was in danger.

If only the end of the tunnel would come soon. The idea that someone would follow him was terrifying. Even with his immense magical power, he couldn't protect her. Not for certain. And what they needed now was speed, not distractions.

* * *

ALONG THE WAY, KORDON NOTICED SEVERAL RUPTURES IN THE tunnel's walls. They were small naturally formed holes that let in the air from the large complex of underground caves. Despite its possible toxicity it provided a better option than no air at all.

He couldn't count the miles he walked, it had to be many. Surely by then they had to be passing under the massive mountain range that spread toward the north.

Soon he ran out of things to think about. His mind felt blank. There was nothing but silence inside his head. No more wondering, no realizing, no shock. Now it was only the dark corridor in front of him, constantly coming toward and passing him by.

Despite the fatigue, he fought to rush on, always imagining that someone would run out of the darkness behind him and attack them. He wanted to run away from it. The more he ran, the more he became afraid that the shadows would form into an enemy and end it all. His breath grew faster, the speed almost amazing in these conditions. He ran as fast as he could without looking back. He felt tears on his cheeks. *You won't take me, you won't take her, you won't take our freedom*, he thought.

With a complete lack of any attention to the floor, he tripped over a loose rock and fell. In the two seconds he had before landing, he instinctively pushed Dianne on top of him. She landed softly on his back while his face hit the dirt. The bloody scratches itched all across his face. He lifted his head from the ground and looked upon his hands as if in surprise. Then he slowly turned around and embraced Dianne's body.

"I'm so sorry," he uttered through clenched teeth as he held her.

He sat like that for a while, breathing heavily and wiping away the tears running down his cheeks.

"I will get you to safety. I promise," he said and stood up. Then he carefully lifted Dianne back over his shoulder and resumed walking.

The paranoia had lifted, his stride was more sure this time. He fought himself to stay sane. *This darkness,* he thought, *can drive a man crazy. To imagine some nations live like this, impossible.*

Suddenly something brought him back to awareness. He gasped in shock as he realized it might have been a sound, reaching his ears from afar. A voice carried to him through the echo. They were behind him, several of them, as it seemed. The voices were too faint, so far, to determine how close they were. It wasn't possible to identify the words, but he was sure he and Dianne were being followed now. After all those years, it was only natural for him to assume the worst. He wondered if he'd be able to outrun them. Apparently not possible in these conditions. But still, he had to try, for all the right reasons.

He picked up the fastest pace possible and rushed on. He could almost hear fragments of words and even some quick footsteps of armored boots. If they followed him this far, they were surely determined to hunt him down.

Out of nowhere, came a next surprise... the tunnel started rising up.

Kordon's hopes were all pointed toward reaching as high as the tunnel allowed. His legs ached as he tried to keep up the speed, but he didn't give up. There would be time to rest once they get out, or not at all. Either way, there was no point in saving any strength.

He could almost hear their shouts from behind. They have probably spotted his light.

Without any warning, a wooden wall emerged from the darkness before him. He stopped almost in place and laid Dianne on the ground.

A torch hung on the wall next to him. He lit it up and used it to survey the room around him. Beside the room made of stone, he could only see the sturdy wooden obstacle defiantly standing in his way.

He contemplated using his magic to get through. There was no use setting it on fire, the smoke could have choked them both before disintegrating. A shock-wave, on the other hand, could blast some pieces back at them, or worse, collapse the whole tunnel.

He punched the barrier. It barely moved, although Kordon had noticed an iron bar lodged into the hole in the wall that prevented the barrier from opening. Kordon tried removing it, the rust kept it firmly lodged in.

The armored footsteps were almost upon them

now, echoing in the room around him. The whizzing sound made him flinch, a pair of crossbow bolts missed him by an inch. He immediately threw his torch into the darkness before him. It revealed two armored figures moving aside to avoid the fire. The shining outlines in the distance behind them revealed many others.

"I'm sorry I have to do this," Kordon said and raised his hands towards them.

Before they could reload and try again, the air in front of him erupted in an inferno of flames that swirled forward like a tidal wave, engulfing both soldiers and continuing onwards.

Through the agonizing screams Kordon immediately reached behind and pulled one of the bolts out of the wooden barrier. He pushed it into the metal bar that held the barrier in place. It moved, slowly. He put all his strength into it, clenching his teeth, sweat breaking on his forehead, heart pounding like crazy. He felt his muscles expanding, pressing against his skin, being stressed to their maximum.

His patience ran out. He waved his hand in a vertical arc before him and the whole cave cracked and burst into an explosion of rocks flying everywhere ahead of him and upwards. The sunlight hit his eyes like a hammer, blinding him for a moment. He immediately turned back to clear his vision and picked Dianne up.

As they quickly emerged from the hole in a rocky

wall, he heard someone shouting his name. An image of the king's guard had emerged from the dark.

"Kordon!"

The guard reached for him with his armored glove, like a demon striking from the shadows to claim his prey. He almost managed to step out too, but the rocks lifted by Kordon's magic fell back to their place and the whole entrance collapsed into a pile of rocky ruins.

Whoever followed the man here did not know that this would be his grave.

Kordon aimed his hand at the rocky remains to push them even further in but he only summoned a small number of sparkles across his skin.

So it has begun again, he thought. *They cursed this land once more.*

The magic was gone. Now he had to rely only on his own wit.

THE OVERCAST WEATHER LOOMED OVER THE FOREST landscape, the gray clouds slowly crawled across the sky. The sun beyond the mountains could barely reach them. Kordon couldn't see anything but trees in all directions from the mountain wall. He had never ventured to these parts of the kingdom, but he knew that the forests were vast and spanned miles in every direction away from the mountains.

Regardless, it was time to move west. As he set out

on the way, he noticed a building among the trees, just a hundred yards away from the tunnel exit. He found it to be an abandoned farm, very old, by the looks of it. It had to be there for centuries as all its wooden structures already showed signs of decay and much of its equipment was scattered around, rusted, or overgrown.

Nothing grew on the two patches of field near it. A sty and a stable stood next to the residential building in an L-shaped layout. Opposite of the house was a barn, just across a small yard with a small firewood shed attached to its side.

The place felt serene. Only the wind blew through, rustling the blades of grass and the leaves up on the trees. It chimed the chains and hanging equipment around the rugged wooden buildings. Kordon swiped the hair from his face and felt the chilly touch of the moist air, reminding him of the heavy clouds it brought along. He felt the first drops of rain fall upon him.

With no other choice, he headed for the barn. It seemed a better choice than a ramshackle building which used to be a home. The hail came faster than he thought, catching them just before they reached the barn.

Surprisingly, the barn contained plenty of hay inside it. Kordon would've expected it to rot, just like everything else around the farm, but it seemed quite fine. He laid Dianne down by the only solid wall in the barn and caressed her face.

The rain became really heavy, causing a thick fog

that made it impossible to see anything further than fifteen yards. Luckily, it only reached as far as the fence made of crooked branches outlining the bottom of the barn, keeping the inside relatively dry.

The simple wooden roof had only a few holes. They would be safe there until the weather passes or gets worse.

Kordon took a wooden pot that lay tossed by the wall and approached the edge of the barn, just outside of the rain's reach. He caught some rainwater into it and then poured it out to clean it. Once he filled the pot again, he brought it back to Dianne.

She didn't react to the water he poured onto her lips. Her eyes remained closed, body numb. Only her chest kept rising and sinking as she breathed.

What else could he do but wait? There wasn't much time to spare, but she needed to regain consciousness in order to move on. He just sat in the hay next to her, holding her hand, wishing for her to come to. His eyes still watched the weather outside, pondering their situation.

The Curse.

He despised the phenomenon that made him and all the other mages powerless. The Gods brought out the Curse to stop people from using magic. It spread across the surface of the Second Continent everywhere they ruled. Nobody knew how it worked or how they spread it, only that it forced people to live without magic. The official dogma claimed magic to be the source of all suffering and people only used it to harm others. To Kordon, it was the most powerful asset he had to keep the overwhelming number of enemies at bay. Without it, Edenia and all its allies would fall in a short time. Without it, he could not protect his family. Without it, he was but an ordinary man.

But the abuse of magic was the reason for all this, the reason for everyone and everything connected to it to be exiled from Earth.

We deserved it, he heard his conscience in the back of his head. *We did kill each other. And we do it, still.*

He thought of how this place could have looked like when bristling with life. Where did everybody go? Where did the friendly chat vanish to? To where the laughter of the children disappeared? Where did the noise of the busy life go? How did the sounds of the honest work and the voices of the animals stop? Were they also consumed by the war? If they were, many more had yet to come into its hungry maw.

He turned to the right, his stare piercing the dense coverage of the forest. He knew it wasn't empty, creatures lived there which could emerge at any time. Large forested areas such as this had their secrets, dangerous predators among them.

He frowned. It rarely happened to him to be this constricted, having to sit in a place while being called elsewhere. He kept reminding himself that this was the new life he chose. Dianne was his wife and a man doesn't leave his wife in need, no matter the circumstances. *Trust them, they can care of themselves*, he kept thinking of the western kingdoms as if they were his children.

In his mind, Kordon recalled countless betrayals, disputes, hate, abandonment and scorn. In the thousands of years he had seen it all. Now everything was different, now he was truly upset.

The reason, his whole world, now lay in his hand. The hand of the woman he gave himself to, and all those who they produced and were about to produce. He felt it made him vulnerable. He was the mightiest, most powerful man both by magical power and the political influence and now for the first time he had to take on a new role; a husband and a father. It was new. It scared him, but it also gave him hope. This supposed weakness will later become his strength when his family will begin to flourish and wonderful things will come to happen.

A sound of ringing reached his ears through the rain, he turned left to see six figures emerge from the fog. Their armor rang as they approached him, he could already recognize the shape of the new Edenian guard. They followed him and apparently dug their way out of the tunnel.

He stood up and walked up to the edge of the barn, they stopped about five yards from him. One of them came closer.

They kept still as they faced each other, nobody said a word. Kordon stood calmly, watching the raindrops hit the armored warrior before him. He knew why they came and appreciated the opportunity to face them standing up. Although he appeared calm on the outside, in fact, his heart kept racing, making him hide his anxiety by taking long breaths. He was the only thing standing between them and his pregnant wife, just him, without his magic. This fight was going to be very personal, defending the closest person Kordon ever had in a long time. He couldn't see the man's face behind the tiger mask but he could tell his tension as well. It wasn't every day someone would ask you to raise your sword against Kordon Elenius.

Finally, Kordon parted his lips, taking a breath for his next words.

"Did you come to kill me?"

"Yes," answered the man and immediately swung his blade at Kordon.

Kordon stepped back, making the warrior miss his target. In his peripheral vision, he could see the others spread out, making their way to surround him.

To survive, Kordon knew he had to even the odds. With only light armor, he stood no chance against this many, not without magic.

He charged the warrior before he could recover from the swing, hoping to topple him and gain advantage. As he moved forward, the man actually spun around, bringing his shield right into Kordon's face. Kordon, ignoring the pain, grabbed onto the shield and pulled back, making his enemy lose balance, eventually forcing him to go down on the ground. The man tried to roll and as he did, Kordon took the hand holding the sword and bent it towards his chest. With little force, he brought his enemy to the ground, driving the blade straight into the man's throat. Letting him drown in his blood, he picked up the dead man's shield and looked up to see the other guards approaching. They wanted to take him all at once, not taking any chances now that he proved to be their better.

He quickly paced against them, stepping out into the rain. The ground became slippery but he intended to use that when fighting against enemies heavier than him.

They came at him from all sides and he stepped back, drawing out their attacks.

Keep moving, he kept telling himself but deep inside he knew this would not be easy. Despite forcing the guards to make firmer, steadier steps, they had too many advantages over him, especially since the rain didn't get into their eyes and didn't soak into their clothes so easily.

He lunged at the nearest warrior to his left, clashing their shields against one another. The extra force allowed him to gain advantage as he swung at the guard's leg, slashing the part which wasn't protected by the armor. It was too small a victory, however. These men were among the best trained and five of them could easily challenge one man, no matter his experience, in the battle of attrition. All it took was one mistake and everything would be over.

He sidestepped the warrior and pushed him again, this time from behind, sending him towards his fellows.

They regrouped and faced him again as he symbolically swung his blade around, demonstrating his lack of fear.

He let out a terrifying battle cry, so strong it made them all change their stances, expecting him to attack any moment.

And so he did.

The fight changed into fencing, Kordon would attack and block, being careful not to get too close to them as they slowly moved around to flank him. He refused to give up. How he would win the fight, he couldn't tell but he kept looking for openings and mistakes in their movements. They were too far in between and covered each other very well. Being a royal guard, they were taught to fight in a team and even Kordon never thought of fighting against them, a mistake he would not repeat, should he survive.

He decided to look for the advantage of the terrain, starting to retreat among the trees next to the barn, carefully choosing the place from which they would not be able to see Dianne so easily. His hand started to become tired. The rain and the fatigue took their toll on his ageless body. Although he managed to stay out of the harm's way, he fought more with his instinct than being in control of the battle. He could barely tell where his enemies stood.

Suddenly something hit him in the back of his head. One of the guards snuck around the barn, surprising him from behind. Kordon fell to the ground, immediately turning around to cover himself with his shield.

He could tell they knew this was his end, they were getting ready for it.

But he would not close his eyes. He refused to hide from his end.

They stood over him, ready with their swords.

No. Not like this.

As they attacked, he rolled to the side, grabbing one of the guards by his legs, then lifting them up to make him fall over.

He quickly stood up, his sword trained at them.

"Let it be known that I fell standing up," he said and prepared for an attack.

Suddenly, in the corner of his eye, he noticed a large dark object move out of the fog, heading straight for them.

A ferocious black bear, larger than any Kordon had ever seen, took the guards by surprise. It leaped at the nearest warrior, mauling him with such a force that it broke his neck. The remaining guards stepped back, trying to surround the bear, looking for an opening to stab it. The animal would not fall for such a trick and immediately charged at the next enemy, catching his leg in its giant mouth. The man shrieked in pain as the leg broke and separated from the rest of the body. The bear immediately bit into his torso and sank its large teeth into the armor, tearing it to pieces along with the one wearing it.

The remaining guards attempted to stab the bear with their swords which the animal ignored so far. Kordon did not want to stand by and wait to be the next on the menu. He dropped his weapon and, while trying to stay away from the others, looked for a way to get back to his wife.

However, what he saw next, was a rare sight for anyone to see.

The bear stood on its hind legs, now being twice as tall as them. It faced the remaining guards who stepped back while hiding behind their shields. With incredible speed it mauled through the first two guards, throwing them several yards in the air and leaped towards the last one. While still in the air, the animal's mouth opened and didn't stop. The whole upper chest vertically split in half, revealing several rows of teeth and fangs. Like a several meters wide carpet of a hungry maw, it fell on the terrified man and enveloped him, swallowing him whole. There, on the ground, the creature remained, twitching and swelling, letting out crunching sounds.

Kordon hurried to get past this bizarre theater to find his wife back inside the barn. He then held her hand as he knelt next to her.

And waited.

He couldn't hear much through the noise of the rain. He could see the dark shape move around the edges of the barn, heading for the way to enter it as well.

The giant black bear came under the barn roof. Kordon watched it carefully, ready for the worst. The animal appeared peaceful, walking slowly with its head aimed at the ground. Kordon forced himself to remain calm. In his head the infinite scenarios played out on what he would do should the creature attack. None of them had him coming out victorious. The bear approached Dianne, ignoring Kordon completely. It tried to smell her, then paused, perhaps to listen. To Kordon's great relief, the bear turned around and walked several yards to the edge of the barn. There it laid down on a pile of hay with its head aimed towards the outside. Then, in the sound of the rain, it fell asleep, or so it seemed. Kordon closed his eyes and listened, not letting his wife's hand go.

Dianne wouldn't wake up for another half an hour. With every passing minute, Kordon grew more anxious about their predicament. The gravity of the whole situation couldn't be lifted from his mind.

When he finally felt Dianne move a hopeful smile appeared on his face.

He opened his eyes as well, the bear was gone.

"How do you feel?" he asked her gently.

Dianne tried to look around. Apparently, she had no

idea what had happened in the past few hours. "Where?" she asked in confusion.

"We are in the forest north of the mountains. I carried you through an underground escape tunnel. We might have some time before they'll find us again," answered Kordon.

"So... it wasn't a dream. Hanal, they tried to kill us?" asked Dianne.

Kordon nodded.

"Ramon, he... He gave his life for me," she shook her head in regret.

Kordon remembered the man, he admired people who would value the lives of others over their own. He couldn't imagine braver an act than that.

"He was a good man," he nodded. "A hero that set the best example."

Dianne gave the memory a moment of silence before she spoke again.

"What was it all about? How could the others turn on us? They were our friends."

"The prince has deserted us for the gods. They tried to lure us into a trap so that Edenia would be defenseless. They also launched an attack on Harij, trying to catch Samara off-guard," said Kordon.

"I can't believe it. I..." Dianne wasn't able to finish her sentence. The pain had returned.

"How bad is it?" asked Kordon, concerned.

"I... I would be able to walk, I think. It's not as bad as before," said Dianne.

"I will do everything I can to get you to safety. I promise," said Kordon while holding both of her hands.

Dianne smiled at him. "I know. What will we do, then?"

Kordon looked outside. "The rain should pass soon. We can't stay here. We need to travel back to the Edenian kingdoms. You will need to give birth in safety and the kingdoms have to be warned. It is the only option I see now."

Dianne slightly nodded. She tried to stand up, supporting herself with her hands. Kordon immediately helped her get on her feet and made sure she could stand. She tried to take a few steps around, still twitching her eyes in pain, but in the end, she managed to walk on her own.

Kordon watched her in joy. Even though her robe was messy and the circlet wasn't shiny anymore, she was alive and well. Deep down within her beated the heart of a lioness who never gives up. She was a woman he had learned to appreciate. She never had anything to prove to anyone and showed her strength by fighting through whatever hardships came her way.

He gave her the gathered rainwater to drink. It seemed to help her from hunger, but not completely.

Kordon had decided to rummage the farm's remains. He quickly ran through the rain, across the yard and entered the resident building.

It was full of old, decayed, and broken wooden furniture. He saw nothing but mess, as if someone had tried to pillage this place before. The tools were scattered all over the floor and pots were mostly broken. Some of them still had remains of whatever they had once held.

It could've been a very cozy place once, thought Kordon. Living alone, far away from everything, in a self-sustaining farm, that was a peaceful dream he had for centuries. Maybe once the war is won, he would move into this place with his family, or on his own, whatever the future allowed.

There seemed to have been a food storage in the back of the main room. The door had been ripped open violently, shattered into several pieces. Still, that didn't keep Kordon from looking inside. Among the rubble there, he managed to find two pieces of sugar bread. The footprint on them indicated that someone had stepped on them, but some pieces were left completely clean. Kordon separated those parts and kept them in his hands.

Then he returned to the barn and offered the food to Dianne. As she ate, he sat next to her and watched the outside.

"You look very bothered," she said to him.

"I am," admitted Kordon.

"You believed they were your friends and they betrayed you. It must be hard to accept," guessed Dianne.

Kordon looked up to the sky, not saying anything as if he tried to remember.

She was afraid to ask him, not wanting to bring back bad memories.

"They felt hurt and exhausted, claiming to be safer on the Gods' side. They all believed we all fight for peace," he finally said and picked up a flower from the ground.

He smelled it, then tossed it away.

"But how can we have peace when we are just fighting?"

"It's hard to argue with that," admitted Dianne calmly.

"They were right. I only hide behind them and the others on the frontline, letting them bleed for me while I just play politics."

He turned to Dianne.

"My power is far too great to be on the battlefield. It can easily get out of control, I can easily get out of control."

Dianne nodded, she understood. She heard of the story of how Kordon became wounded in battle and went mad. The entire city was destroyed because of that, a stigma he had to bear every day. It reminded him of the consequences should his power get out of control.

"But betrayals hardly surprise me anymore," he continued. "Ever since this war started nothing remained the same for long. Sometimes one person switches sides, sometimes it's a whole kingdom."

"Yet you are bothered now," said Dianne and laid her hand on his. He repaid her with a smile.

"They tried to kill you and our child. I wouldn't forgive them if they succeeded."

"I hope that you didn't have to kill anyone to escape."

"I did and it wasn't easy. They are still our people, even if they decided to forsake our cause."

He looked her in the eyes and she felt the truth in his following words.

"I would have gone back and killed them all should something have happened to you. Down to the last one."

She said nothing. Her silence told Kordon that perhaps he shouldn't have said that, even though she understood.

They sat in silence for a moment.

"Do you want to hurry home?" asked Dianne.

"I want to protect what I value in this world. If we sit here, I can protect nothing. But I don't want to rush you."

"We seem to be adequately safe here, beyond the mountains. Just you and I," smiled Dianne.

Kordon thought of the dead bodies he had to dispose of.

"They know we are here. And this land is now cursed. Without magic we are not safe here."

He let out a long sigh.

"I am just an ordinary man now, powerless."

Dianne could feel how upset he was. She took his hand.

"Kordon, look at me."

He did as she asked.

"Even without magic, you are more than an ordinary man. You kept us alive thus far, have little more faith in yourself," she reminded him.

It made Kordon think, his wife was right. So why couldn't he take his mind off the task at hand? Was he really so obsessed with having the situation under control? Couldn't he just stop worrying for a moment? It was much easier before they had children together, when he just worried about a faceless nation than a person so close to him. The difference between those two situations felt crushing.

"No matter how strong I am, there is still a risk they might get to you anyways. I don't want that to happen," said Kordon.

Dianne smiled. "Maybe you'll feel better if I sing for you. Do you remember the song In the Future?"

Kordon chuckled. "You're welcome to try."

Dianne started without warning. The song was slow with its tones rising and falling like a ride on the ocean waves.

"Over the days, your heart will find a place. Further away, there it shall stay. Still beating strong, never be wrong. In eternity you will find solitude, kindness and gratitude. Only I know what the future will hold, but it's not for you to be told. If you hold my hand, next to me stand, you will find why our love will never die."

Kordon smiled back at her and joined her. "So leave your trouble behind, spread your wings wide, begin your journey. Tomorrow gives you a chance to sing, rejoice, dance, make things better, rewrite your past to the last letter. Stand up and run, always look ahead, don't ever step back. You can't lose, only gain. It's there in the future, a world without pain."

As the song came to an end, Dianne pointed outside. "Look, it's about to stop raining. Finally we can go."

Kordon, completely submerged into the song and its meaning, took a moment to react. He stood up and approached the fence. It indeed seemed as if the rain was about to stop soon. The clouds began to retreat and the morning sun brought back color and sharp contrast to the world.

"Can you walk?" he asked Dianne.

Instead of answering, she stood up. "For you, for the baby," she said and exhaled heavily. Still, she would hold onto his hand.

So they departed. There was no road that would lead to the west. Striding in the wet grass proved difficult, especially for Dianne's high-heel boots, but there was no other way.

Soon after, the air became hot again. The sun rose up quickly and the forest animals sometimes ran across. If it hadn't been for the pressure, it would've been a nice leisurely walk through the forest. Kordon paid no mind to the nature around him, though. In his mind, it was dimmed and chaotic. He let Dianne walk a step ahead so he would always have her in his sight.

* * *

It wasn't until noon that they arrived at the forest's edge. The trees started to fade away and only patches of grass remained, scattered across rusty dirt. The barren land stretched all over the horizon. The cloudless sky loomed over it, empty, save for a giant round spot of blinding light that scorched the land below.

"How will we ever make it?" asked Dianne.

"We have to avoid the big road and keep going forward. Then, over the plains, we have to walk until we reach Nammon. I'm sorry, but it's the only way," said Kordon.

Dianne grabbed his arm. "It's alright. As long as I'm with you, I have nothing to worry about." She gave Kordon a long kiss.

Soon the forest and the mountains behind them disappeared and became only a fading memory replaced by another barren horizon. They walked for a long time without a single rest.

Suddenly, Dianne stumbled and would have fallen if Kordon hadn't caught her just in time.

"Are you well? We can stop here if you need some rest," he offered.

Dianne just shook her head. "No, I'm just... My head hurts. It's so warm. The sun is burning me."

Kordon looked up, nearly blinded by the unpleasant intensity of the sun and the blue sky hosted very few small clouds on the horizon.

They both fell victim to the torture of the heat. Kordon knelt next to his wife and laid her onto his lap. He unstrapped the plate of armor he wore on his chest and used it to cast shadow over his wife's head while trying to shield the rest of her body with his own.

"I'm responsible for all of this, and look how little I can do for others without magic," he said in shame.

Dianne smiled at him.

"I trust you," she said calmly. The look in her eyes told her it was true. The sheer belief, kindness and honesty felt overwhelming to him.

Despite the searing pain caused by the burning skin on his back, he felt touched by this. He knew he had the trust of the people he led, but nobody told him with such honesty that they trusted him. And especially in that moment, he felt that the trust was misplaced, that he could not follow on that trust, even though he had promised it during the wedding. Ah, the wedding, what a great event that was throughout all of the world. Nobody would have ever had thought someone such as him would marry at all, let alone to a person who had no magic whatsoever. He told everyone that Dianne was the one he had been waiting for all his long life, but that was only the half of the truth.

Dianne took him out of his thoughts, running her hand across his rugged, sweat covered cheek, smearing the dust left by the wind. She continued up into his messy, dirty hair to swipe it from his tired face. She pulled him closer and lifted herself up a little to kiss him on the lips. Even though their bodies suffered from dehydration, the touch of her lips felt like an explosion of fresh energy. It sent buzz into his whole body that left him with nothing but calm and peace.

He saw the reflection of his eyes in hers. They lit up, not just like any other person's when they became happy, but actually became bright blue. They sparkled like the clearest sea under the azure, cloudless summer sky. He actually felt the corners of his lips lift up, without an effort, as if his body reacted by itself to hers. He felt his negative thoughts recede into the darkness in the back of his mind. He now felt as if he were in a whole different space.

Suddenly, something caught Dianne's attention. She pointed somewhere nearby. Kordon looked that way and saw a piece of shiny metal object sticking out of the ground. He knelt next to it and picked it up.

"It's a silver shard. Some places here have bedrock made of it."

He showed it to Dianne, she seemed to be quite surprised. He didn't realize why that was until he turned it around. It had several markings etched into it. It looked as if someone had tried to bite through it.

"I wonder who has teeth strong enough to do this."

He kept analyzing the shard. It was about four inches long and curved like a claw. There was apparently a story behind this item, but nothing that would seem too obvious. He threw the shard away and nodded at Dianne to let her know they were moving on.

They slowly paced across the barren desert, struggling to keep themselves upright as to not hunch over and fall in exhaustion. The sun above their heads did not seem to move at all and Kordon kept his armor above Dianne's head to keep her covered. He would never give up hope. However, their bodies could only go so far and eventually started to reach their limits. It had seemed the bitter end was at hand until the heat waves on the horizon revealed an amorphous object. Hardly distinctive so far, it rather resembled a dark gray smudge. Yet there was definitely a hope for an oasis or other place possibly offering shelter.

As they approached what had revealed itself as a solitary vegetation area, they found a carcass, half-buried in the dirt. It belonged to a large feline animal, its head measuring twice the size of Kordon's. It apparently died in a fight, as it laid on its back and was missing one leg. The unusual thing about this beast was that it had many parts of its body still intact. The marks on what used to be flesh indicated someone or something had attempted to bite it. The structure of the carcass left them both puzzled. The entire body apparently had an orange fur-skin with a silvery green tone, making it look statuesque. It was definitely a living being once.

Kordon knelt next to it and reached for its remains. Suddenly, the dirt before him exploded and he caught just a mere glimpse of a black carapace, before dodging the powerful outburst.

He turned around to see a giant scorpion emerge from the cloud of sand. It stood nearly eight feet tall and as it turned around, he could see its ruby red eyes watching him.

In the corner of his eye, he could see Dianne attempting to hurry to the oasis. The animal recognized her as an easier prey and turned around to charge at her.

Kordon ran up to the monster and used the talon he had found earlier to stab at it. It barely managed to pierce a lower part of its tail. Still, it was enough to alert the animal and reconsider its priorities. It spun around, bringing its giant pincer to get rid of him.

Kordon jumped back, hoping to avoid being hit. With not enough time and distance, the pincer smashed into his chest armor, making him fly several yards back. He rolled on the ground and remained lying there.

Believing this was the end of it, the scorpion turned back towards the oasis and picked up an incredible speed.

Kordon stood up and picked up a nearby rock the size of a fist.

"I'm not finished with you yet!" he shouted and threw the rock with all his strength at the scorpion.

To his surprise, the rock took off in the form of a flaming trail, as if he had thrown a meteoroid. It flew straight through the monster's tail, leaving a burning hole.

I can use my magic here, flashed through his mind.

He ducked and swung his hand just an inch above the ground.

A shockwave that he created caught up with the scorpion and hit its legs, bringing it down to the ground.

Kordon quickly looked to Dianne. She was about halfway to the oasis.

"Keep running, don't stop!" he shouted after her.

The scorpion lifted itself back onto its legs in no time. Its body parts suddenly started to spin and separate until its carapace unfolded into nearly double its previous size.

This giant monster leaped at Kordon with an amazing speed. He tried to react with his magic, but a swing of a giant pincer knocked him away. He flew through the air and fell to the ground. The clothes on his back ripped apart, submerging him in the discomfort of bloody scratches. Ignoring the pain, he looked up to see the animal standing still in the place where it landed.

To his surprise, the scorpion turned around, and headed toward the oasis. He immediately lifted his hand up again but then halted himself when he realized he could also hit Dianne if the attack was too powerful. He decided to do the only thing he could do; run after it.

Dianne just managed to reach the oasis and started looking for a place to hide. She didn't look back. There were no chances she was willing to take. The monster followed her, even as she made her way through the line of trees that outlined the oasis. Its hulking size slowed it down as it had to make its own way. With every broken tree came another obstacle that had to be overcome, but it wouldn't stop a hungry giant scorpion.

Kordon finally managed to catch up with the slowed animal, but the broken branches blocked his approach. He had to go around, guessing that Dianne was headed toward the northern part of the oasis.

There he saw a ruin of a three stories tall tower made of sandstone. A part of the building was still intact, although two walls had collapsed. It would still provide a useful place for Dianne to hide.

Kordon ran through the grass and avoided the remains of what appeared to be an old camp. Wooden boxes and iron tools were left behind to decay, all broken and useless. After running through the tree line behind the camp, he could finally see the whole tower before him.

Dianne had just reached the tower, with the scorpion being merely ten feet behind her. She ran through a small opening in the broken wall and then disappeared from Kordon's sight.

The scorpion rammed the wall with its pincers, making the whole structure shake. A couple of rocks fell down through the showers of dust and sand.

As it continued ramming, Kordon picked up the nearest stick he could find and broke it in half to make a sharp edge. When he looked up again, he saw the tower finally collapsing to the ground. The beast had backed off a bit to avoid the falling debris.

Kordon prayed to good fortune that Dianne would have made it out without harm. It was time to step in and save her.

He finally managed to get into a good range to grab the animal's attention. It wasn't that hard, one more rock carefully aimed at its head was enough to get noticed.

Unable to locate its previous prey, the scorpion turned around to face Kordon. It was only about a hundred feet between them, too little to guess what to do.

Kordon lifted the stick up and waved it in the air. A mass of magical force began to accumulate around it. With all his strength, he threw the stick at the charging scorpion's head. Like a bolt of lightning, the stick hit its target, but bounced off of the thick carapace and continued onward to pierce through the lifted tail.

Green blood started pouring out of the wound and the monster let out a painful stuttering roar.

Although the wound didn't stop it, Kordon didn't have to care about Dianne being nearby now. He spread out his arms and quickly thrust them forward. A lightning arc slashed through the air directly in front of him and hit the scorpion. The monster twitched and spasmed as it became enveloped in a net of pulsating electricity. Kordon could hear its painful scream through the cracking and boiling of the soft body. When he finished, there was only a giant carapace left, with remains of burned tissue on the inside.

Kordon passed the smoking shell and quickly approached the ruin. Dianne was nowhere to be found. Silence fell upon the oasis. Only the wind ran through the grass and trees. After checking around the ruins, he found footsteps of Dianne's high-heel boots in the dirt. They led around the rocky hill. Kordon followed them until he spotted his wife ahead, among the trees. She looked exhausted and leaned against a tree.

"Dianne!" he shouted after her. She noticed him and with a smile on her lips, she slightly waved her hand at him. Kordon didn't need more than ten seconds to hold her in his arms again.

"It's gone now," he said calmly.

"Thank you," she replied.

Kordon looked around.

"Are you well?" he asked.

"Yes. I'm quite hungry, though," she said.

"Let's search around. We must find something useful," suggested Kordon.

Around the hill, they found an abandoned mining camp. It seemed as if the miners didn't care about packing anything or taking it away. All the mining equipment was still in place, only it all looked so decayed. The gray tents were torn and covered with dust and the rusty tools lay tossed around on the ground.

Some of the wagons still contained the remains of the mineral. It looked like silver but something felt strangely odd about it. The thick substance gave his skin a vibrating sensation as he moved it around in his fingers.

The wind waved his hair in the air as he surveyed his surroundings. With a disappointed look on his face, letting out a sigh. "We are not going to find any food left behind."

Dianne took his hand with a sorrowful expression on her face. "I don't know if I can keep going like this, Kordon. The baby will want to get out soon, I can feel it."

Kordon laid his other hand on hers. "Please don't stress. I will get us to safety, I promise."

Dianne smiled. "I believe you. But not even you can foresee the future. I'm worried that something might happen to you and you won't be able to fulfill the promise."

Kordon didn't know what to say. Indeed, he never questioned his mortality. And he never felt obliged to prove to others whether he could die or not. Neither Samara nor Danub were ever willing to put that idea to the test, which gave rise to wild rumors and speculations about the Three.

"If that should happen, I will fight to the last breath to protect you and our baby," he said and embraced Dianne.

"I know," she acknowledged with a calm voice.

As Kordon looked ahead, he saw a small lake at the center of the oasis. The pressure of the underwater currents had to create it or possibly there was an impenetrable bedrock beneath, reinforced by the silver.

When Kordon and Dianne approached it, they couldn't tell whether the lake was made artificially or not. Time covered any obvious marks.

Kordon helped Dianne drink some of the water, using only his hands he had cupped together. He couldn't trust any of the pots left behind, as the risk of poisoning by rust or rot was too high.

They both rejoiced for the discovery that the trees growing in the inner layer of the oasis carried fruit. Not much of the brown pear-like fruit could be found, but it was easy to reach and peel. The joy, however, didn't last for long.

Just as Kordon managed to shake the second bunch of the fruit from the tree, the wind carried over a sign of new problems.

"What was it?" asked Dianne.

"It sounded like a roar of some beast," assumed Kordon.

"Another scorpion?"

Kordon shook his head. "I'm afraid to guess."

Without any further words, he ran toward the direction where the sound came from, the eastern edge of the oasis. There on the horizon, he beheld a painful sight.

A large army had been marching in his direction, logically, as it had to travel from water to water if it wished to cross the barrens.

The biggest problem of all literally hung in the air above the ground. A menacing shape of a giant monster levitated over the heads of all the enemy soldiers. It was still too far to see the details, but Kordon already knew what it was. The long twisted body and waving tentacles could not be mistaken for anything else.

Dianne was still finishing her fourth fruit while Kordon came in, running like the desert wind.

"The army of the gods is coming our way," he said, and helped his wife to stand again.

"Already? So they finally caught up with us?" Dianne asked in surprise.

Kordon shook his head. "No, it's an invasion army. We need to hide somewhere. I'm sure they are coming this way and will stay here for a while."

They both headed to the north, toward the cave.

"What do you mean by...?" asked Dianne, but suddenly stopped when she noticed the incoming army through the opening in the trees. "Oh, the good fortune! What is it?" Her mouth and eyes opened wide, she pointed at the animate object floating above the ground in the distance.

"There is no time. If they see us, our chance to hide will be low," said Kordon as he continued to pull Dianne toward the cave.

They both entered the mining tunnel. The entrance had already been overgrown with bushes and trees and when Kordon collapsed it with his magical power, nobody could tell there was any way in anymore.

3
DEPTHS

It was dark now. Kordon couldn't even see his own hands in front of his face.

"What do we do now?" he heard Dianne's voice next to him.

"Now we have to explore this mine," answered Kordon as he lifted his magical light.

Thin veins of silver shimmered along the tunnel walls. The light revealed more equipment scattered throughout the tunnels, and to Dianne's horror, even corpses of the miners.

She leaned closer, observing their torn thick leather outfits and rotten flesh hanging from their yellow stained bones.

"Is this normal? No signs of being eaten by rats or worms. The bodies simply decayed as they decomposed," said Dianne, puzzled.

"Something must have killed them or chased them

out. But it's difficult to tell anything beyond that," speculated Kordon.

"There are at least a dozen of them," said Dianne in marvel.

Kordon took note of a rack with full metal helmets. They covered the whole head, leaving only a narrow slit to see through.

"They wanted to protect themselves from something inside," he pondered.

The web of tunnels took them deeper into the underground until they emerged in a large cave shaped like a dome. Most of its texture was covered with silver, which reflected the light very strongly, so Kordon didn't need to use such powerful magic anymore.

While Dianne admired the view, Kordon gently sat her down on a big flat rock.

He looked around and saw two other exits from the cave in the northern and southern walls. They were both caved in. The cave's western part gently formed into another tunnel. It didn't look like it was mined. There were no wooden or metal supports and the walls were smooth, almost organic in their shape.

"What was that thing outside?" Dianne's voice echoed around the cave and disappeared in the tunnels. Kordon sat next to her.

"It was a giant mehai," he said plainly.

Dianne shook her hand in disbelief. "Mehai? Giant? I thought they were a sort of water squid. And how come it was flying?"

"Some of them can be bred to grow into any desired size. It takes a long time and it doesn't happen often, but it is possible. Mehai use their ventral sacks to launch themselves from water to attack prey outside it. The giant ones can use this ability to fly with practically no limits."

Dianne still couldn't hide her surprise. "So they've brought a colossal monster to attack us? How do you kill something like that?"

Kordon exhaled in frustration. "If one of those things drops on an unprepared city, it's over. Throughout my life, I have seen many kinds of monstrosities, worse than mehai. Any of them can still be brought to life."

Dianne looked as if she would faint. Kordon immediately held her around her chest.

"Rest, my love. I will think of what to do next."

Dianne looked into his eyes. "What is there to do? We are trapped inside a cave. We don't even know what's happening outside. If the army leaves, we simply won't know."

Kordon looked to the other end of the cave. "The tunnels lead deeper underground. Maybe they exit somewhere far away on the surface."

"Then let's go," suggested Dianne, as she tried to get up, but a painful look on her face betrayed her unease. She was reaching beyond her limits. Kordon gently held her down, preventing her from standing up again.

"Stay here. It might be too dangerous. If I find something in there, I will come back for you."

Dianne tried to resist. "Would you leave me here in an empty cave without a light?"

This dilemma made Kordon clench his teeth in frustration. "It might turn out to be a futile effort. I just don't want you to get tired for nothing."

Dianne didn't say anything. Both of them sat in silence for a while.

Kordon looked up. "How deep are we?" He thought of making a hole in the ceiling to let the light and air in, but he could feel they were too deep to do that. And then he finally made the decision.

"Let me help you up." Kordon carefully helped Dianne stand up. "You are right. I can't leave you here."

Dianne smiled at him. "Many sun cycles ago, I swore to follow you, even to the bitter end. If we are to face hardships down here, we do it together."

Slowly but surely, Kordon led his wife with the help of his light. The tunnels descended further into the underground and even there, the corpses of the miners could be found.

After a while, the corridor emerged in another large cave. It was quite narrow, but Kordon couldn't see the bottom or the other end. The slim and treacherous path seemed to have stretched over the pylons rising from the infinite depths. It was crooked and sometimes giant stone arches rose above it. There were no signs of artificial workmanship. Everything seemed to be formed naturally.

Kordon stopped and listened. As Dianne curiously stared at him, he closed his eyes and focused. A sound echoed through the cave. It might have been the wind or perhaps even a river. It didn't mean much, but it still made him feel more comfortable than silence. Without any words, they resumed their journey.

After about a mile of the tiresome trip, a cave wall emerged from the darkness. A small and narrow entrance opened the wall, promising a way further. A broken wooden frame lay on a plateau before it.

Yet the biggest surprise came in the form of a miner's corpse. It seemed to have been broken in half and laid on two wooden boxes. In its hand, Kordon found two red crystals of rough spherical shape. They were both dim by now.

"Dear," he heard Dianne speak. "It doesn't seem as if it will ever lead us up. It is as if…"

Her voice faded into a noise coming from behind her. Kordon focused back into the darkness and an incoming wind lifted his hair. A dim light appeared in the far distance. It seemed to have been moving.

"Stand behind me!" he shouted through the noise, and walked onto the walkway before Dianne.

He could now see the two red lights shining brighter and closing in on him, while slowly spinning over the walkway and under it. Kordon couldn't tell what it was as it stayed outside his light. Through the wind, he could hear a roar, almost like a beast. He spread out his arms, which both still bore his magical light. Dianne had turned around and crouched behind him. Kordon waited until the monster revealed itself.

Into the light, emerged a serpent with an immaterial body. It continued spiraling toward him, a creature made of wind, with the ruby eyes being its only solid part. It didn't seem to react any different as it was closing in. It just slowly repeated its motion around the walkway, with the roaring noise being louder and louder.

As it came closer, its real size finally became apparent. The creature's head was nearly as big as Kordon himself. He threw his hands forward, as if pushing the air with his palms. A massive light barrier lit up before him. It bent backwards slightly as the serpent crashed into it head on.

Kordon could feel the pressure, powerful and relentless. To him, it would compare to pushing against a train. Now that the wind creature had stopped in place, the whole walkway began to shake. Small rocks began to chip away at first. Kordon realized that the rock was breaking apart. The serpent had stopped and split in half. It tried to get around the barrier from both sides and assault Kordon. But it was too late. The walkway had broken and both Kordon and Dianne fell into the darkness.

* * *

When Kordon woke up, he felt pain throughout his entire body. Centuries of hard body training had hardened his bones enough for them to not break upon the fall. His muscles, however, felt weak and sore. The cold stone stung his skin as he touched the ground. It became clear that they were still inside the cave.

He tried to get up quickly and his skin lit up with magic, but the pain made him break back down and it was dark again. The least he could do was wave his arm in the air, to have at least a bit of his magic light. Even this little sufficed to light up the whole cave around them. The silver veins surrounding them reflected it even further, thus outlining the shape of the cave.

It seemed as if they fell about two floors down, onto a wide flat plateau. The pieces of broken walkway lay scattered around and the subtle noise of water roared somewhere near. He could hear Dianne gasp next to him. There she was, on her back, motionless.

"Dianne, are you hurt?" He quickly crawled close to her. Fresh blood poured across her lips.

"The pain," she let out softly through clenched teeth.

Kordon grabbed her hands, he could feel her react back. Dianne started to cough, as more blood came out of her mouth. Kordon immediately helped her to turn sideways so she wouldn't choke. He tried to wipe the rest of the blood from her face. Her skin felt so different now, rather rough and strong.

Upon closer look, Kordon could see that the tissue

had changed in some places and started showing a weave of silver strings. *Radiation*, he immediately thought. That was the cause of the burning sensation he felt on his skin since they entered the cave. This silver must be somehow poisoning them. Dianne, in her weakened state, was very vulnerable at the time.

"Kordon," she said. "I can't feel my legs."

Kordon looked at her in horror. "How is the baby? Can you still feel it?"

Dianne put both her hands on her belly. Her eyes opened wide. "It doesn't move." She turned her face away from him to hide the tears.

"What will we do now?" she asked.

Kordon tried to lift her upper body up and embrace her, which only made her cough up more blood. "I don't know. Your back has been broken. I can't move you without any help."

He felt Dianne's hand firmly grab his arm, pulling it toward her. "Kordon, you must save the baby. Cut it out of me, if you have to."

Kordon shook his head. "No, if it hasn't died already, then it's best for it to stay inside. The radiation would kill it fast."

Dianne tried to pull herself toward him. "We can't just... Ooooh!" Her eyes opened wide in shock from the pain.

"What is it?" asked Kordon while desperately trying to support her upper body with his hands.

"The baby, it's moving. I can feel it. It wants to be born," she said while panting heavily.

"Are you sure?" asked Kordon in surprise.

Dianne quickly nodded. That was pleasant news for Kordon, and so he helped her to lay against the rocky wall. Her belly had already been bumping into her robe as the baby moved inside.

"Will you manage?" he asked her.

Dianne violently shook her head. "I can't push. It wants out but I can't..." Her speech cut into a shocking scream. "But it still hurts! Oh it hurts so badly! It needs to get out!"

She grabbed Kordon's hand. Even this little gesture gave her more strength to fight on.

"Kordon, if I don't survive this, please make sure our children are safe. Do not let them die in this war. Make sure they grow up into strong and beautiful people."

Kordon just shook his head again.

"You have been through this before. You can make it," he reassured her. In his mind he found that hard to believe, the logic dictated otherwise. There was a very little chance of surviving this situation. Even though he wished it to be the contrary.

"No, if I don't push it out it will stay there and die."

Kordon looked at Dianne's lower body. There was already blood on her robe. The birth had indeed started. But it needed two to finish it.

"What can I do?" He witnessed some births in his

long lifetime, but he was never a part of the process. Now the situation changed and he needed to improvise.

"I... I can't. My head feels..." Dianne fell unconscious. The grasp on Kordon's hand stopped.

"Dianne!" shouted Kordon and held onto her head. He tried to put his thumb on her eyelid and push it open but all he could see underneath was emptiness. Her eyes had already fallen victim to the silver which spread over them like a spider's web. She wasn't there anymore.

"Dianne! Can you hear me? Dianne, wake up!" He tried to gently shake her to bring her back to consciousness, but it was a futile effort. It seemed as if her breathing had stopped too. Any signs of life had vanished.

The baby! Kordon quickly put his hand on her belly, and to his relief, he could still feel the baby moving inside. It wanted out, it had to. Staying inside was certain death.

"Push it out," said Kordon to himself. But how? He couldn't tell. He was capable of great destruction, his magical powers were strong enough for that. But bringing life into the world?

Then he realized, magic was the only power he could use to help. It had to be possible somehow. But only the most skilled magicians could harness such power to perform a sensitive task such as pushing a baby out of a womb. Nobody could match Kordon's skill with magic in this world, millenia of practice made sure of that.

He moved his hands over his wife's belly. While holding his hands still in the air, he made a gentle push and his hands became covered in a gray glow. The invisible force pressed against the body. Kordon carefully and slowly waved his hands over the belly, as if he were touching it. Nothing had changed so far. He tried to push harder. The bump under the belly finally moved. He continued while sometimes stopping to make sure the baby wouldn't be crushed as it passed over the hip bone.

It pained him to wonder if Dianne could still feel anything. The pain must have been horrible if she did. But he could not prevent it at the moment. He had already lost her, he wouldn't lose the baby too. "Don't die on me, please."

The baby became stuck, it wouldn't move any further. Kordon broke a sweat on his forehead, but wouldn't ease the pressure. Something was wrong, it made him afraid. His heart rate increased as he fought to keep his hands from shaking. Was it really possible to push the baby without its cooperation? He didn't know much about female anatomy to be sure. But there were no other options. Either he would try to push it out himself or it was over.

He finally decided to apply more force. Surprisingly, it seemed to have worked. The bump on the stomach had begun to lower itself and Kordon could hear the scream of the newborn baby coming from underneath its mother's robe. It lived, such wonderful news! Kordon's mind was flooded with relief.

But they haven't won yet. Kordon continued pushing until the bump disappeared. Dianne's robe had turned completely red in its lower part. Kordon pulled the robe up and reached between Dianne's legs. From there, he managed to pull the tiny creature out and showed it to the world. It was slippery and hard to hold with only one hand, but in the end, it managed to rest comfortably on top of Kordon's palm.

He looked at it carefully. "A second daughter," he gasped. Perhaps he was not meant to have the son he had hoped for. But now that he had lost one woman in his life, he was grateful for another.

One last problem remained; the umbilical cord. Kordon knew it had to be cut, which wasn't as easy to do as it seemed. Unfortunately, he didn't have any sharp instrument on him. Perhaps Dianne... His eyes rested upon the top of her circlet. He took it from her head with his glowing hand and knelt before her spread legs. Then he laid the baby on his knees and held the cord with his left hand while using the circlet as a makeshift knife to sever it.

Once that was done, Kordon stood up. Proudly, he held his newborn daughter. "I humbly ask you to be the shining star of my life like your mother was," he proclaimed with a smile.

He sat down next to Dianne and showed her the child. She would not move. Only a lifeless body remained behind. Nevertheless, he placed the baby into an embrace of her hands to let them share at least one touch.

"I am so sorry this had to happen. I wish you could forgive me," he said with tears in his eyes. "My life has always been dangerous. Being one of the most powerful and longest living men wasn't as easy as it should've been. I used to think my power could protect the ones I loved, but I was wrong. I have seen countless people die, many of whom I have seen being born as well. Still, I am grateful for your love and the time I had spent with you. It was one of the brightest chapters of my life." Then he took his vest off and wrapped the baby in it. After laying it carefully onto the ground, he threw the remaining placenta into the dark depths and put the circlet back on Dianne's head.

He decided to leave Dianne in that place. Her body would be safe there. There was no way he could get her out quickly enough to save the baby from dying. He put the body onto a sloping silver rock, with her hands crossed on her chest. As she rested there, peacefully as if in a coffin, he approached her with the baby in his hands.

"I promise one day I will come back for you," he said, and kissed her on the cheek one last time.

The serenity of the scene was interrupted by the baby's cry. Kordon looked down upon it.

"We can't stay here."

4
BREAKING OUT

The land shook in its foundations as the rocky wall exploded. Its pieces flew across the camp. They crushed and smashed everything in their way, be it people or equipment. There were indeed many soldiers around, all shocked by this unwelcome tremor.

Nearly all of them wore black and orange armor, the striking claw symbol of Harunai kingdom proudly painted on their chests.

Out of the dust cloud of the crumbling entrance emerged Kordon. He walked as surely as a man determined to overcome any obstacle and watched their surprised faces with contempt.

Awestruck, nobody knew what to think of his presence. Obviously, they didn't know him, or at least what he looked like.

Among the soldiers stood one dressed in light leather armor with a deep blue plate on his chest.

Kordon recognized him as the captain of the Hanal army. The man recognized him too. His eyes and mouth opened wide in surprise.

Kordon stopped and looked around at each and every one of the soldiers.

"I wouldn't grin if I were you," said Kordon to the captain, seeing as his facial expression changed suddenly.

"Pleasure to meet you again, Kordon Elenius. It's generous to deliver yourself to our hands so willingly," said the captain and chuckled a little.

"I suggest you leave this place while you still can, or I will remove you myself," said Kordon in all seriousness.

"You think we're afraid of you?" said the Captain mockingly. "We will never let you leave, or your wife, who I presume is hiding in the cave."

Kordon saw all the soldiers readying their weapons as they took their first steps towards him.

"So be it."

He quickly spread his hands and... nothing happened. Everyone stopped, waiting what would happen. Kordon looked at his hands, feeling the familiar buzz just under his skin which told him the energy would not come out, the Curse prevented it from manifesting once again.

"The Gods have already cursed this land, Kordon," laughed the captain. "Not even you can overcome it. You are at our mercy now."

Kordon himself didn't appear bothered, however. He glared at the soldiers surrounding him, his fists clenched. Even if they somehow managed to spread the Curse to this place, he would not give them the satisfaction. They didn't know what he was really capable of. No one did.

"You don't know anything, young one," he said and slowly began to raise his hands before him.

As he started to bring his open palms closer to his chest, his face started showing the signs of struggle. He would narrow his eyes and clenched his teeth like a bodybuilder attempting to lift a great weight. Sparks of magic appeared at his fingertips, only briefly, dying before they could separate from his body as if some unnatural wind had blown them away.

Before the very sights of all the witnesses a net of magical energy spread across his body, glowing through his skin and clothes. Kordon collapsed to his knees; more and more light consumed his body and shone from his eyes.

Awestruck, everyone took a step back in fear.

"How is this possible? The Curse prevents all magic!" asked the captain, shocked by the unbelievable vision.

"Put him down!" he shouted to his soldiers while pointing at Kordon.

The soldiers immediately approached Kordon with their swords, ready to strike. As soon as their blades struck Kordon's body, they shattered to pieces and their hot shards flew through the air, knocking everyone back.

Kordon let out a terrifying roar and the whole world around him came alive in a maelstrom of wind and everything caught up in it.

As soon as the captain saw that, he immediately turned around and ran, followed by his comrades.

They never got far. The energy exploded from Kordon's body and the whole world disappeared in white light.

The light faded away and the magic dust dispersed in the wind. Kordon lay in the middle of a fifty yard wide circle of dead ground covered only in burnt rocks. The dust slowly settled down, mixed with particles of ash – a remainder of everything living that used to be there.

He felt his heart beat fast, hammering against his chest as he tried to catch breath. He breathed in some of the dust and coughed it out. The place returned to its serene state, only Kordon made a sound as he tried to lift himself back on his feet. Casting magic always took its toll on every mage, some more and some less. It was not common for one such as him to suffer from this effect, but the struggle against the Curse exhausted even his immortal body. He struggled and fell before finally managing to put himself upright.

A baby's cry reached his ears. He turned to the cave entrance and walked back in. He found his second born daughter lying on a rock nearby, in pain and vulnerable.

He lifted the babe carefully and smiled as he looked upon it.

"Not a welcome into the world I would like you to have, my dear. I hope that your life will be much better than this."

Kordon didn't have parents, not like everyone else. He saw people raise their children but never had done it himself. He had hoped Dianne would be the one tending to the girls while he would provide for them. What would become of the girls now? He had no idea and that scared him. To lead the world took an incredible amount of effort, let alone care for someone in a constant need for attention.

He looked to the west towards Edenia, his home. With his perfect eyes he could see shapes in the distance of the army that just passed through. Clearly, someone had noticed his display of power and sent a unit to see what all that was about.

"We have not much time. Let us go. I swear to you, I will protect you for as long as I live."

They left the oasis to the south.

5
BLACK ARRIVAL

"Cherry! Don't get too close to the edge!" shouted Marla as she rushed toward a careless little girl. She caught her just in the nick of time. The little one would have otherwise fallen down.

They stood on a platform overlooking a beautiful port city of Farhamn in Edenia. This platform was a part of a large luxury villa made of white stone. It was decorated with many plants and flags to break up the winds that flew across the mountain range upon which the villa stood. The sun shone bright that day and one could see the sea glitter all the way from there, even the few miles from the coast.

"But I wanna see mommy and daddy when they arrive. They have been gone for so long!" insisted the girl as she wiped her golden blonde hair from her face to reveal an angry frown. A golden sea bird would land on a table close to her. Annoyed, she scared it away.

"I know, but if you want to be alive by then, you'd better stay away from the edge," said Marla, carrying the little girl further back toward the building.

"Can we at least go to the port? Being here is so boring and I can't wait," begged the girl.

"Why? They will be coming here eventually. Be patient."

But the girl just set her big blue eyes at her. "Please. I really wanna go. Please?"

Marla sighed. The girl would not give up. The idea of leaving the empty house for the much livelier port overflowing with people was too strong. "Oh Cherry, what does it take to make you happy?" Then she nodded in agreement.

"Yay!" cheered the girl as she jumped in the air. Then she turned around and ran into the house.

When she ran out, she held a clay pot in her hands, almost as big as her head. Three flowers grew in it. They were of the same family, but their petals had different colors.

"Now what is this?" asked Marla curiously.

"Mommy told me that picking flowers up kills them, so I dug them up and planted them here. I was growing them by myself in the backyard and I wanted to give them to mommy and daddy when they arrive." Then she waved her hand as a signal for Marla to lean closer. When she did, the girl lifted the pot almost into her face.

"See, there are three flowers. One is for mommy,

one is for daddy, and the last one is for me. We are a happy family, just like the flowers. They will always stay together." Marla smiled and took the pot into her hands.

"Now let us go," announced the girl, pointing at the gate.

* * *

IT HAD BEEN A YEAR SINCE KORDON AND DIANNE LEFT FOR the Second Continent. The war broke out again, the whole world was mobilized and neither Kordon nor his wife were seen in Edenia since. Life in the kingdom was undisturbed, however. The modern technology and its location provided enough comfort and peace for the locals, far from the war. Although as usual, it was only a matter of time before the enemy would find its way here as well.

Farhamn stretched along the entire coastline of the bay. Everyone wanted to live as close to the water as possible so they could go and sunbathe on the beach or sail around on flatboats with tall sails. Being situated on the eastern shore of Edenia, the sun would rise up directly above the water, making for some amazing sunrise. Many people visited the city in the summer, making the streets crowded and noisy. People wearing colorful outfits filled the areas among the white walls of the broad streets.

In fact, people would mingle as far as the eye could

see. The unending chaos of voices sometimes diminished under the piercing cry of a siren coming from the port. Upon each step, one could smell fresh restaurant food that fought for dominance with people's perfumes. The town itself had flourished over its long history. People came to see some of the oldest buildings in Edenia that dated to only a decade after the arrival of mages on Sentia. It was a paradise for tourists who enjoyed the local hotels, inns, restaurants, or shops that offered curious souvenirs.

Even an older woman like Marla liked to visit Farhamn, simply to reminisce on her youth, before she became a caretaker for many important families in the kingdom, before she would become a kind older lady.

The little girl, however, didn't pay any attention to that. Being only five years old, everything felt new and wonderful to her in this busy city. Her keen sense on details made her absorb everything she saw. She marveled at the food stalls in the main arcade and the strange animals that some of those people had as pets. But perhaps the most amazing to her, were the street magicians. Even though they had only little magic about them, they amazed the audience with both illusionary tricks and real magic, sometimes making it difficult for the bystanders to tell the two apart.

Marla, along with the little girl, passed by the harbor area of the town. Many dock workers spent their time fishing after the hard shift of loading and unloading the numerous cargo ships.

But this was not the end of their journey. The main destination was the hoverport on the other side of the city. Its building stood five stories tall and all the surroundings reflected in its highly polished metallic walls. It was situated right by the end of the beach, on the northern edge of the city. The landing platforms extended themselves over the water. A small number of hovercrafts had already landed, but the most important one, which the girl had so eagerly anticipated, was still missing.

They both sat on the bench by the building and watched for the incoming traffic. "That one, over there!" The little girl pointed at the sky. Marla looked that way, but didn't see anything but a group of clouds. "That cloud looks like a train," said the girl when she noticed Marla's clueless stare. Really, now that she looked again, it did resemble a train. The clouds were lined up in a row, and the first one was the biggest.

Suddenly, a hovercraft emerged from one of them and disturbed the peaceful drift. They both watched as it landed on one of the platforms and after the whirlwind around it dissipated, the vehicle's hatch opened.

"That is them, isn't it?" asked the girl, excited. Marla shrugged. It was hard to tell from where they sat.

"How about I go and take a look?" she asked.

"Yes, please," agreed the girl. Then she watched as Marla ventured all the way to the hovercraft.

She seemed to have been talking to someone inside until they came out. It was Kordon. He spoke to a woman who followed him out, holding a baby in her hands.

"Daddy!" the girl shouted, running to him.

When she finally managed to reach him, she noticed Marla's surprised expression on her face. But that didn't spoil the joy of the moment for her. "Daddy! I missed you so much! Don't ever leave me again!" She grabbed onto his leg and would not let go.

Kordon bowed down. "Wealla! There is my little girl," he said as he caressed her hair with his hand.

Wealla looked at the woman who accompanied Kordon. She looked nothing like Dianne, her hair was brown, had a round face and was much shorter.

"Daddy, where is mommy? I want to see her too," she asked and looked around.

Kordon deeply exhaled. He and Marla exchanged glances. Then he looked into the ground and shook his head. She gasped and put her hand on her mouth. Seeing their unhappy looks made even Wealla's excitement start to fade.

"Wealla, I have some bad news. There has been an accident. Your mother didn't survive the birth. She is gone."

Kordon made an attempt to make his voice as calm and peaceful as possible to avoid distressing her. He could not tell if he succeeded.

The girl's eyes and mouth opened wide.

"Gone? To where? You can't mean... You mean she is not coming home? Ever again?"

"I'm afraid so," confirmed Kordon.

"This is so horrible," said Marla with tears already running down her cheeks. She tried to bow down and comfort Wealla, who only pushed her away. Instead, the girl stepped up to Kordon, grabbing him by the waist as she looked up at him.

"That can't be true! Please, daddy, tell me it's a joke! We wanted to go out together. I waited so long!" she urged him.

"I'm sorry. She died while giving birth. Wealla, meet your new sister, Silveria." Kordon took the baby from the woman standing next to him and lowered it down so that Wealla could see it.

The sorrow on Wealla's face changed for anger. "I don't want any sister! I want my mommy! Do you see this?" She lifted the pot up. "This was us! You, me and mommy! Now this has no meaning!"

Upon that Wealla turned around and ran away from the platform. Nobody tried to chase her. They knew she needed to be alone for a moment.

Wealla stopped at the edge of a low stone wall near a pier. "Mommy is dead," rang in her head. More than as thoughts, she heard it as a voice echoing inside her mind until she realized it came out through her own lips.

That can't be true!

She took the pot and tossed it into the water.

Her head was spinning as she watched it sink and slowly disappear from her sight. Breathing became heavy for her, she felt pressure on her chest. Wealla didn't know what to do. He said that if someone dies, they are gone forever. She would never see her mother again.

Why?

Dianne was the most precious person in the world. The one that always cared for her, been there for her, showed her that the world was a good place. Now who would bring her peace, scare away the demons in her head?

Suddenly, she felt so lonely. Even in this heat, the world around her grew cold. Her legs gave up. She tried to hold onto something, but instead stumbled as if driven by a whirlwind. Such a long time had she waited for her mother, only to learn it had been in vain. Dianne was not coming back. Nothing she could do would change that.

How did it happen? Who did it? Mommy!

The image of Dianne smiling at her, rose before her eyes. It slowly faded into the sky. Wealla's eyes became filled with tears as she reached out for it. She longed to touch her mother one more time. Being held by Dianne was her greatest desire at the moment.

But the picture had faded completely, swept away like dust in the wind. She watched it with an empty stare for a moment. Then she simply lowered her head and clenched her teeth in a painful grin. The anger burned inside her. But there was nowhere to direct it. She had to contain it inside.

Her eyes flashed bright as a result of this stress. The girl wasn't yet aware of the magical energy inherited from her parents. However small it was, its presence couldn't be denied. Dianne used to own a small amount of magical energy, as it was with many people in the world, although she never let anybody know as it was barely worth mentioning. Wealla was theoretically able to do magic on a slightly smaller scale. Without proper training, however, she was not aware of what she was doing. That is what happened. In anger, Wealla burned her eyes with magic. The energy ripped through the iris and let blood in, changing its color forever. Since she was still so small, it was able to affect her greatly.

It hurted.

She twitched her head in pain and tried to rub her eyes, but it didn't help. In loss of perception, she stepped right over the edge and fell into the water.

Darkness slowly swallowed her. In this empty void, she tried to summon back the feeling of her mother being nearby. It was no longer possible.

The next thing she felt was Kordon's hands holding her. As she opened her eyes, she found herself back on the stone wall and her dress was still wet from the water. Kordon knelt in front of her and Marla stood next to him. They both looked worried.

"Daddy, this is not good," she said, still in grief as she kept smearing water and wet hair from her face.

"What has happened to you, darling?" asked

Kordon. He knew she was referring to Dianne's death, but now he was concerned about something else.

"I fell," she said plainly, without looking at either of them.

"Cherry, your eyes," gasped Marla. She took a small pocket mirror from her handbag and handed it over to Wealla.

The girl looked upon her own reflection in the mirror and saw the change in her eye color. The eyes that were once sky blue now turned dark red. She let out a frightened shriek.

Kordon lifted her up into his embrace. "It will be alright, my daughter. It will be alright," he reassured her.

EPILOGUE

Thus ends the story of Silveria's birth. Kordon Elenius might be the most powerful mage on Sentia and certainly have the wisdom of ages, but nothing could ever have prepared him for what was to come. Alone, he would face the struggle of being a single parent having to raise two daughters. How can he, as a man, understand the mentality and the needs of a child of an opposite sex? What effect will the absence of a mother have on the family?

Many challenges lie ahead for the Elenius family, and they will all be tested beyond their limits. As nobles, they will have to live up to the family's name and what is expected of them. But there is also war, the lethal and vicious war from which no one can hide.

ABOUT THE AUTHOR

Tomas grew up in a small town in Eastern Bohemia, where not much of anything happened. Raised as a bilingual, he started absorbing all kinds of stories both from his country and abroad. Eventually at the age of 14 he started writing stories to express his emotions and view of the world. By eighteen he finished writing his first novel in Czech language before permanently switching to English language. As he moved through life and around the world he created or co-created several other media projects, inspired by his own life and the lives of others. Tomas writes exclusively in his free time.

Tomas has traveled extensively around Europe in search of understanding its history and visited the USA on several occasions. He also lived in Sweden for a couple of years. When he isn't traveling abroad, he loves cruising the roads of his home country in his stylish convertible and enjoying the beautiful countryside.

Besides writing, Tomas enjoys various artistic pursuits such as traditional and digital painting, video making and photography, playing electric guitar and piano and even took a course in opera singing. He is also an experienced dancer and wine lover.

Tomas lives in Prague.

Check his website at tomasburian.com for more information on his books.

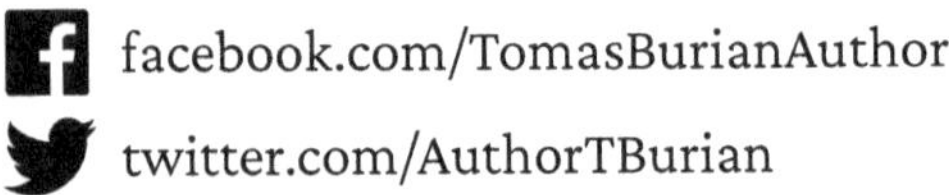